JOURNEYS
INTO DARKNESS
AND LIGHT

BY

ANDRÉ NGUYỄN VĂN CHÂU

© Copyright 2015 Journeys into Darkness and Light
by Andre Nguyen Van Chau

ISBN 978-1-941345-53-5 Hardback

ISBN 978-1-941345-52-8 Paperback

eISBN 9781310861888

AISN B00W1W0JNI

Library of Congress Cataloging in Publication Data
Main entry under title: Journeys into Darkness and Light
Library of Congress Control Number: 2015938399

ERIN GO BRAGH
Publishing

www.ErinGoBraghPublishing.com

To the memory of Catarina Pham Thi Vang

my Mother

And

To Sagrario Barbillo Van Chau

my love, my comrade-in-arms and my wife

Table of Contents

Solitary Confinement

After he had convinced me to write his official biography I had interviewed the Archbishop hundreds of times. I had spent numerous days in the narrow guest room of his cluttered apartment in the complex of Palazzo San Callisto (an extraterritorial property of the Holy See) in Rome to go over the minutest detail he told me. Yet there still were dark areas that we left for later, even those that might be most essential to his life. It was like blank spaces on an almost finished canvas. His visit to Geneva where I used to live and work was to fill one of those blanks.

Three days ago the first rhododendron blossoms burst open. Now the air of the entire Parc de la Grange was heavy with the dizzying fragrance of thousands of the bluish bushes. It still was a challenge to lie in shirt-sleeves on the grass as winter had not retreated entirely from Geneva; but the young sun did what it could to dispel the remaining gusts of cold wind.

We were in shirt-sleeves, and we were on the grass. The luxury of doing casual things, like lying on the grass, seemed to be a treat for my friend, the Archbishop. He was enjoying it tremendously to be out in the open, there in the park with young and old strangers walking by and around us.

We looked up into the cloudless sky. At a distance, from the far side of the park came the humming of spotted

1

doves. Beyond the fence of the park, the rumble of weekend traffic became indistinct and unreal.

He said, continuing in his familiar monotone: "That time they put me in solitary confinement for almost four years. When the wardens wanted or were ordered to break the resistance of a prisoner they put him in solitary confinement. I was isolated from the world around me. I was totally "forgotten" by the rest of humanity. Little by little life was drained out of my body and mind. Time stopped flying; and moments masqueraded as eternity. I missed the sounds of human voice. I missed them so much that at night sometimes I dreamt of being insulted and cursed, kicked and cursed, beaten and cursed; and oh, in the morning I woke up happy...happy for a long while, and hoped that the dream would come back often. The kicking, cursing and beating were blessings compared with complete isolation."

He stopped and turned to me: "I wish you would never know what real loneliness is."

How many times had he talked to me about the days he was with other prisoners around him? Some of those co-prisoners had been released earlier and had told me anecdotes about the time they spent with him. They all had told me that at meals, he always gave most of his portions to others and that he always volunteered for the most back-breaking and most humiliating tasks, such as cleaning the latrines and carrying baskets of human feces over long distances. They had talked to me about his taking any insults and any violence from the wardens with calm and humility.

Apparently, those days with other prisoners were blissful days compared with the months without human faces and human voices.

He went on with his narrative and I did not need to take notes. I knew I would remember word for word what he said.

"You have to be my biographer." Oh, I remembered, and regretted how foolish it was for me to have accepted his request one windy night on a beach near Rome! Was it Anzio? Or was it in Sperlonga, or maybe Fregene? Though I had fought valiantly against the honor; I had succumbed in the end to his entreaties. He was my friend and I should not have hesitated a second to be his biographer, if the narrative was limited to his life, his family, his trajectory from parish priest to Bishop, then to Coadjutor Archbishop of Saigon, and his thirteen-year-long imprisonment. But how could one write his story without dipping into his spirituality? I was scared to death to touch that part of his life. And one couldn't handle *his* biography without his relationship with God! His spirituality was even more important to him than his life. But, how could a layman like me touch that part of him? He had said hardheadedly: "You must be able to write about my spirituality: you are my father confessor". Yes he said that, but I was no father confessor, and opening my eyes as wide as I could, I only got glimpses of the depths in his soul.

He said: "I know. I know that you have suffered too. But I was in a cell scarcely larger than two square yards, with no window, no light. There was no bed, no table and no chair in the cell. There were only an old straw mat, a damp and moldy blanket and a wooden pillow. A rotten door would swing open into a hall twice a day to allow me to use the toilets at the end of the hall. I could not see who opened the door and who closed it. Food on a tin plate was pushed into my cell once a day; it was slid in through the bottom plank of the door. Once the plate was in my cell, the bottom plank was slammed back into place. Of course, the same ritual took place when I finished eating. An empty tray would be slid in. It would slide out with my empty plate on it."

"I found a crevice under the door on the first day I was in the cell: I was covered with sweat after a few hours in the hot narrow cell in midsummer and I could hardly breathe. Then I found a little ray of yellow light under the door. I pressed my face hard against the rough floor and the crack under the door and was able to breathe. The little crack however was not large enough for me to see anything outside the cell. It allowed me nevertheless to distinguish day from night: the light was yellow at night, as it came from a kerosene lamp in the hall, and it was a little brighter in day time when the sun was up. It also allowed the visits of some little insects."

I knew he was starving at the time, and knew what he would do to the little visitors but I decidedly did not want him to tell me how many roaches and how many crickets he had consumed raw in those miserable days. I cut him off and reminded him: "So, Your Grace, you said life was drained out of your body and mind; I want to hear more about how your mind failed at the end."

He frowned, perhaps irritated by my impatience. He remained quiet for a long while, then choosing his words carefully, he said: "It was in the third year of solitary confinement. One night, I knelt down to say my evening prayers as usual. All of a sudden, the sky fell and the world went spinning and spinning and spinning. *I could not remember one single prayer.*"

I asked: "Did you actually lose your memory all of a sudden?"

He shook his head emphatically: "As you know I had a great memory since childhood. People said that I had a photographic memory. In prison we all understood that we needed to nurture our memory for survival: every day we had to write a confession. We had to remember every word that we had put on paper the first time. If in any subsequent confession

4

we changed a word, a simple word, then they would question our truthfulness and interrogate us until we collapsed. No, we trained ourselves to remember. Memory was our plank of salvation. But that was a long time ago before the episode I am talking about. Nobody asked me anything; nobody interrogated me anymore for over two years. Darkness penetrated my mind little by little. Loneliness and the dampness of the cell seeped into my soul. Soon enough the darkness inside me blotted out all the joys I had found in the world, all the smiles I had seen, all the beauty of nature, leaving me with only remorse and self-contempt."

He was shivering and I threw over him the long grey shawl he had discarded earlier. Distinctly over the rumors of the traffic beyond the fence of the park, I heard the sounds of the Lake Leman water assaulting the black rocks on its shore.

He sighed: "The world inside me was fading away, like the faces, the flowers and the trees in an old photograph. Everything was fading, faster and faster, until all was gone. I tried to fight back. I focused on the details of some memories and laughed at times when I scored a handful of little victories against forgetfulness.

"But I knew I was losing the war. Every day and every night forgetfulness advanced into me, loomed over me. Darkness closed in pitilessly. Then, that night I knew that the defeat was total and that "they" would soon discover that I had lost my mind. Then even that terrible knowledge also faded away."

*

He sank back into silence. People told me that after a long stretch of solitary confinement even an introvert would become talkative. This however was not an illustration of that claim. He continued to be a man of few words. Though he was in a way dictating his biography to me, he was not talkative. Sometimes he sat brooding for hours, wasting precious time, as I had to fly south to Rome or he had to fly north to Geneva whenever we could meet for short whiles.

He was shaking as he stared at me. And I could feel the horror that seized him and dragged him once more step by step into the depths of hell, into something far worse than death.

I reminded him softly: "Yet, remember that you came out of there alive, Your Grace!"

He closed his eyes, snapped out of his terror and said: "Yes, I did survive. Let me tell you how and why...Unconsciousness would have been a blessing! No, I lay there sprawling on the straw mat, acutely aware that I was immured in a wall of silence where even the throbbing sounds of heartbeats had disappeared. I was aware that I was in hell and that hell was the absence of all. As I said, I lay sprawling on the straw mat, for how long? I didn't know. But all of a sudden some gurgling sounds came out of my throat: "*Eloi, Eloi, lema sabachtani"* I gasped :" What was that? what did I say? Am I completely insane now? Does any of this make sense?" Little by little I distinctly heard the whirring of my brain that started working again. Yes, I know the meaning of that scream. *My God, my God why have your forsaken me?* the words muttered by Jesus in agony, dying on the cross. Blood, hot blood rushed to my brain, started a drumbeat at my temples. My head was about to explode. But the terror was gone, hell was gone, the emptiness was gone. I remembered well Psalm 22, having turned it again and again in my mind throughout my ordeal until now. No it wasn't a scream of despair. It was a beautiful psalm ending with *Posterity will serve Him ; future generations will be told about the Lord, and proclaim His deliverance to a people yet unborn, saying that He has done it."*

His voice trailed and I looked away. Several seagulls made useless circles over the manicured lawn of the park where the tiniest fish and the tiniest bread crumb was absent.

He cleared his voice and said: " I still could not believe that the recovery of my memory was real. I felt that except for Psalm 22 a dense fog still covered all the prayers I had learnt from childhood. But then, from the midst of the fog came out "Eva", "Eva" ! I wondered why *Eva,* then some of the fog dissipated and I heard myself say *"Ave".* All my body shook and I cried as I knelt up and said three *Ave Maria* in a row. As tears ran over my hollowed cheeks the joy in me exploded and I stood up, drunk with a sense of victory I sang aloud the only song of victory I knew, the *Te Deum".*

We looked at each other and laughed for a while. Yes, we both remembered how on rare occasions we had sung the *Te Deum* and made the stained glass windows of our seminary chapel tremble. It was a long time ago when blossoms of Chinese flowering apple formed fragrant arches over our paths; when pungent ripe fruit half-eaten by bats in the orchards made seminarians dizzy; when short days were devoted to prayers and intellectual exercises and long nights were filled with glorious dreams. In those days in An Ninh Minor Seminary, the rare festive moments when we sang *Te Deum* were the most memorable.*

His face was radiant now, like when he was very young. He said: " I sang until the guards came in and asked me to stop singing so loud. I knew that they knew I would never be defeated or destroyed. The next day they threw me temporarily into a large room with around fifty other prisoners. Long solitary confinement wasn't behind me yet. Because after a few days they led me to another narrow cell again. But I had no fear this time. My few days with other inmates galvanized me. I took into me their voices, their faces, their worries and their laughter. I took all that treasure into me. Those memories would be there with me for a long time. I was no longer afraid of another spell of solitary confinement."

He asked, as if challenging me: " Wasn't *that* a miracle?"

Five years later, when his official biography that I wrote, *The Miracle of Hope",* was in print, he died from a rare form of cancer resulting from a couple of botched surgeries done during his thirteen years of imprisonment. He died within a year of his elevation to Cardinal. As the Church calls him a *Servant of God* and starts the long process of beatification, the image of his moment of utter despair in a narrow cell stops giving me pain. A shaft of light from somewhere penetrates that cell bathing him with peace and igniting his exultation, and he keeps singing:

Te Deum laudámus: te Dominum confitémur.
Te ætérnum Patrem omnis terra venerátur.

We praise thee, O God:
we acknowledge thee to be the Lord.
All the earth doth worship thee:
the Father everlasting.

And forever in my mind the stained glass windows of our seminary chapel keep trembling.

* *An Ninh Minor Seminary only lives in the memory of those who spent wonderful days there. It has disappeared from the earth by evil enchantment. In 2009 a group of former seminarians went back there to see whether any thing remained of the magnificent buildings, orchards and botanic gardens. They reported back quoting Mark: " Not one stone left standing on another."*

8

A Public Execution

The parishioners including those who normally attended mass at remote missions and sub parishes gathered at main Gia Hoi parish church on that Sunday. They had been summoned there by messengers of the pastor who had not revealed the reasons for the summoning.

The pastor, Fr. Thong, was fearless in his homilies. He showed courage again and again as he preached against some of the restrictive measures taken by the revolutionary government. By doing so he galvanized the spirit of the majority of his parishioners but alienated a number among them who believed in the new rulers.

He was tall, broad-shouldered, but emaciated. His skin was sallow as if he suffered from a chronic illness. But his eyes were bright, his gestures well-controlled and he spoke with a clear and deep voice.

Everybody knew he was a member of the imperial family and that he descended directly from Emperor Minh Mang, his great-great-grandfather. That did not mean anything much with Hueans, as the city population included an inordinate number of *tôn thất,* or members of the imperial household. What was extraordinary was that he descended also from the Blessed Tong Viet Buong, a martyr, killed by Emperor Minh Mang. The Blessed Tong Viet Buong was Fr. Thong's great-great-grandfather on his mother's side.

9

Was he the only one person who was not worried? We wondered. At least at the beginning of the revolutionary government rule, everybody else in Catholic communities in the North and in Central Vietnam seemed to be worried. They huddled inside or near their churches and talked in whispers about the upcoming persecution.

There was nothing strange in the fact that they were worried: Their grandfathers and forefathers had been victims of persecutions under the emperors and over a hundred thousand Catholics had been slaughtered from the sixteenth to the nineteenth centuries.

But this time, in 1946, besides the worries, more and more visibly, a tidal wave of frustration and anger swept across the Catholic parishes in Hue and also in other towns and provinces.

The Catholics were fully aware of the dangers inherent to their joining the *National Catholic League*, an entity that existed at first only in name. Yet they flocked into its ranks proclaiming more and more loudly that they wanted national unity and solidarity not fratricidal wars among the patriotic parties, that they would not accept materialism and atheism and that the revolutionary government should listen to the will of the people instead of the dictates of the Komintern.

To the intimidation campaign fomented by the new authorities -- It was not uncommon that kids threw stones at Catholic going to church on Sundays – the pastor responded by recommending that three times a day, as soon as we heard the sounds of the Angelus bells, Catholic adults and kids would go down on their knees even when we were in the street, to recite aloud *"The Angel of the Lord declared to Mary: And she conceived of the Holy Spirit. Hail Mary..."* For us, from the elders to the young kids, the kneeling and the praying in the street represented an act of defiance, a way to say: "We are not afraid." The population of Hue understood that the defiance was not only directed against the authorities but also against our own fear, when we knelt down to pray the *Angelus* in the street. That was why no one threw stones at us when we were on our knees.

On that Sunday, the fact that the pastor convened them without telling them what they should expect put the parishioners on edge. But here they assembled and prayed ardently in the old and beautiful Gia Hoi Church, waiting for the moment when the pastor would ascend the ornately carved wooden pulpit and tell them what he had in mind.

*

The Sunday Mass was conducted quietly until it was time for the homily. From his pulpit, the pastor faced his parishioners in silence for a couple of minutes. Then he said: "Yesterday I was allowed by the revolutionary authorities to go to the Citadel jail and talk to a political prisoner. He had wished to become a Christian before his public execution next Friday."

The Citadel jail under the old regime was merely a small police detention center under the jurisdiction of the Admiral Protector of the Imperial Citadel who, contrary to his grand title, commanded only two squads of famished on-call militiamen since the French turned Central Vietnam into a Protectorate sixty years earlier. He himself was never armed and had obviously no military skills. Contrary to many of his arrogant colleagues, he was kind, gentle and sensitive. He chose to be loved rather than feared. The detention center, a part of his sprawling residence and offices, had certainly never served as death row.

Many village mayors of the Citadel's ten *villages (thập phường)* had been gently and routinely thrown into that center

11

for appearing at the morning briefing of the Admiral with too visible signs of a hangover. After they came out of there on the same day they would laugh and tell us how the Admiral had come in and talked to them kindly about the harm of alcoholism and then had released them and thanked them for their "good work".

Since the August Revolution, the Admiral Protector of the Citadel had vanished. Nobody among the people of the *ten villages* dared mention his name and the revolutionary authorities never told the people what happened to him or who replaced him. The Citadel on-call militiamen had all gone home and the scared village mayors seemed to have stopped drinking rice wine.

With the revolution, things had taken a more serious turn. Indeed, some people kept saying – contradicted by facts-- that dogs had stopped barking and roosters had stopped crowing.

*

We sat with frozen faces as we learned for the first time that the harmless detention center had become a jail from which people might be escorted to their place of public execution.

There had been a well-known place for public executions near the An Hoa Gate southwest of the Citadel. It occupied a small flat field facing the foot of the Citadel defensive walls. In the distant past, murderers, and burglars who had dared to slip into the Imperial palace and laid hand on its treasures were routinely beheaded there when caught. More recently Vietnamese patriots were executed there not by order of the emperors but by the French: Tran Cao Van and five of his comrades were decapitated there after their attempt to restore Vietnam's independence under Emperor Duy Tan failed.

"What are the authorities thinking? To execute a political opponent on the same spot where the French had executed six of our national heroes? Wasn't the place consecrated by the blood of Patriot Tran Cao Van and his companions?"

The pastor said: "I came prepared: I mean, I had my purple stole and a small vial of holy water with me. I came prepared because the authorities had told me in advance that the prisoner might want to become Catholic. So, I told him I could baptize him right there in his cell."

The pastor was suddenly shaken by an overwhelming emotion; he struggled for a few seconds then went on:" But the young man shyly asked: "If I am baptized here, in this jail, how could my baptism become a glorification of God?" I was taken aback. I asked him: "Then where and when do you want to be baptized." He smiled and said: "At the execution place, right before *they s*hoot me."

"What he said stunned me and I objected: "That would be high melodrama and I don't want to play any part in it." But shy as he seemed to be, he stood his ground against my objections. In fact, I was not fighting him too hard because I didn't believe that the authorities would allow such a thing to take place. But somehow he was persuasive enough that I, as well as the authorities, relented. So, you hear, this young man who a month ago did not know anything about Christianity wants to glorify God by entering his Church just before his execution and in front of the public. What do you think?"

Since his arrival at the parish Fr. Thong had introduced unorthodox practices such as allowing questions and answers during his homilies.

We looked at him and were concerned. He looked frail and sickly. When he stood at his ornate pulpit to deliver his homilies, we were afraid that he would faint and never recover after pronouncing passionate homilies. We were afraid for his security, as revolutionaries among his parishioners had warned that someday he would be "taken down".

The parishioners were silent for a long time. Then a young voice shouted out: "We will all go to the execution!" Other shouts followed: "We will bear witness to his courage!"

The pastor said after the tumult died down: "No, remember that he is no martyr. Make sure you understand that point. He is going to be executed for being a member of the Quốc Dân Đảng, a Party that opposes the revolutionary government. It is all right if you want to come to the place of execution and *pray for him and with him.* But please don't act like you are witnessing the death of a martyr. And please, don't bring your children with you."

*

Once the mass ended, parishioners streamed out of the church into its front yard. The pastor headed toward a small group who talked very loudly about the dangers of having a *reactionary* as pastor. One of the men in the group, with a revolver in his belt was waving his hand and shouted: "Why do you idiots side with a traitor who deserves to be executed? Why?"

Young people in the other groups responded by shouting back: "You idiots! You will be the next victims of the new regime. Don't you understand that?"

The pastor shook his head and raising his voice, he said: "You still are on the church ground so, please, do not start a political debate here. We are not *for t*he man condemned to

14

death, we are not *against* him. If we go to the execution place, it will be because we want *to pray for him and pray with him before he dies*. We are not opposing the revolutionary authorities and we do not condemn the people's tribunal that doled out the death sentence. We are to be united in thought and in action. Go home peacefully. And may God be with you in the trying days ahead of us."

He turned to the man with the revolver: "You will not carry a weapon into the church ever again. You were in the secret police under the French, then under the Japanese, and you are in the secret police again now with the new authorities. Remember that we all will pray for you too."

*

Thousands of citizens of the Citadel streamed towards the place of execution. A very large crowd carried banners that read "Death to the traitors!" "Down with the Quốc Dân Đảng!" and red flags with a yellow star arrived first and occupied two levels on the terraced rampart. That crowd included a few groups of pre-teen kids in Vanguard Youth uniform. A far smaller crowd arrived a little later and stood quite close to the first group on the wall. The second crowd did not carry banners or flags. They held ostensibly their rosaries and chanted their prayers softly. A few children accompanied them in spite of the pastor's advice not to let the children come.

They had to wait a long time before the condemned man was brought to the place of execution and instructed to march in between two rows of armed soldiers. The pastor walked next to the young man. They came to a stop where a pole had been erected. Next to the pole there was a table draped in purple cloth and displaying a bottle of holy water, a vessel of anointing oil, a chalice and a goblet of mass wine.

A strong wind blew the gowns of spectators, and made the yellow-star bright red flags of the new regime flutter.

The clacking and fluttering noises of the flags did not cover entirely the rumbles of the *De profundis* that rose and fell like the tide advancing and retreating on a beach.

The crowd stood against the battlements of the Citadel Walls looking down to the execution pole and the intricate ceremonies performed by the pastor as the young man received one after the other the Sacraments of baptism, confession, first communion, confirmation and anointing of the sick.

An officer finally stood up and read out the death sentence. His voice was at times buried in the hurrahs and the grumbles of the crowd. But we could hear bits of the sentence: *He* is a traitor; *he* works against the revolution, *he* has conducted major sabotage operations and *he* deserves to be punished by the people. He has been sentenced to death by the People's Tribunal."

The young man was allowed to say some words and he spoke succinctly: "I am innocent. My only crime has been to be a patriot and a revolutionary. My love for the people of Vietnam and my love for our motherland will live on long after my death. May God forgive those who kill me today because they do not know what they do." Then he shouted "Long Live Viet Nam!" and we shouted after him "Long Live Viet Nam!" Strangely enough, the people who carried banners calling him "traitor" also shouted: "Long Live Viet Nam"

He refused the bandage *they* offered him and looked calmly as the platoon of executioners took aim at him. They shot two salvos as none of the bullets of the first salvo hit him. After the second salvo his body sagged against the ropes that tied him to the execution pole.

An officer stepped up to him and shot him once in the right temple.

The executed young man was dragged out of the scene and loaded onto an old truck.

Some in the crowd ran to the execution pole. Some among the crowd pulled out their handkerchiefs and dipped them in the pools of blood on the ground. The pastor on his knees and deep in prayer looked up and muttered "Don't do that! *He* is a believer, not a martyr!"

*

Many months later, with a bunch of kids, I went back to the spot where the young man was shot. It was a sunny day. All the traces of the public execution were gone. But his voice still shouted "Long live Viet Nam!" and the voice of the crowd still rang:" Long live Viet Nam". The age-old walls of the Citadel echoed back: "Long...long live...live...Viet Nam...Viet Nam".

Did he die? Yes he did. I saw how his crumpled body was dragged away and thrown into the back of a truck. Like a slaughtered animal. But, for me, on that day, running and jumping with other kids, I understood for the first time the exclamation in the Letter of the Corinthians: "Where, O Death is your victory? Where, O Death is your sting?"

*

Two years later Fr. Thong fell into a trap *someone* laboriously laid out for him. One of his most talented and devoted assistants for charity work happened to be one of the most beautiful women in Hue. She funded and managed almost single-handedly a soup kitchen for the young and the poor. People were never embarrassed to come and eat lunch at her Youth Activity Center. She used to serve for a while then

17

would take a tray of food and sit down at one of the three long tables where over a hundred sat and ate at a time. Because of her beauty, and because everybody knew that she donated most of the fund, people treated her like a queen. But when she sat down and ate, she did so like a trencherman. She seemed to enjoy the lunch like everybody else. We called her simply *"the Lady"*.

*

The possibility that someday the pastor would be taken away or taken down was real. A few assassinations of prominent Catholics made it clear that one should not exclude a scenario where the pastor would be killed in full daylight or at night. The pastor always opened the door personally, day or night, if he heard someone knock at the door of his rectory.

Toward seven one evening, a disheveled young man rushed into the house of *the Lady* and stammered: *"They killed the pastor. He is dead."*

She ran to her car and drove to the church. She stopped the car and ran to the rectory. She knocked at the door and waited. She was stunned when she heard the voice of the pastor come from inside: "Just a minute, please."

The door opened and both the pastor and she knew that they had fallen into a trap. They stood, unable to make a move. Suddenly, they were dazzled by camera flashes and brutal yells: "We caught you red handed! Adulteress and lewd priest! We caught you red handed!"

The pastor held the trembling hand of the lady and escorted her to her car through the small angry crowd that continued to spit invectives at them and take pictures of them. He waited until the lady's car turned into the street safely. Then he headed back into the rectory without saying a word.

18

*

Though innocent of any wrongdoing, he voluntarily asked the Bishop to send him to a monastery where he would spend his time meditating and praying. Though I still was very young, I came to see him as often as I could. I brought him the news of his parishioners. He listened attentively, inquiring after each and everyone. He rarely laughed. But he seemed to embrace his new life without bitterness. He spoke about the past without regret and without resentment. He had a vice though: he never had the courage to kick the habit of water pipe smoking. But other than that he lived like a saint.

In his cell, cluttered with books, he had enough space on a wall to hang two paintings: one, dressed in imperial garbs, was his paternal great-great grandfather, Emperor Minh Mang; the other, in military garbs, a sword pointing to the ground, and a halo over his head, was his maternal great-great grandfather, the Blessed Tong Viet Buong, Martyr. Sometimes he waved his hand at the two paintings and said with ironic merriment: "My paternal great-great grandfather killed my maternal great-great-grandfather. Yes, my paternal great-great grandfather was a great Confucian scholar who believed that Christianity was "spreading darkness in his empire and corrupting the hearts of men". He became a methodical in implacable persecutor of Christians. My maternal great-great grandfather was a loyal Commander of the Imperial Guards who obeyed any order of his emperor, but refused to disavow his faith. He was imprisoned, tortured and beheaded. He is now a Blessed Martyr."*

Looking into my eyes he said:" Remember, always remember that we descend from generations of martyrs. Three hundred years of persecution accounted for more than a hundred thousand Christians condemned to death, sometimes to horrible death."

He nodded his head and said: "Be proud of the fact that you are the heir of a hundred thousand heroes'.

*

Seventeen years after the historic public execution and fifteen years after he fell into a trap, Fr. Thong was buried alive by order emanated from unworthy sons of Hue during the *Tet Mau Than* Offensive. When we unburied him, we found a crumpled piece of paper in the pocket of his cassock. On the paper, written in haste, only one short sentence: "May God forgive those who are about to kill me today because they do not know what they are doing."

We did not have time to linger on him. There were other shallow graves to find, bodies to unbury and weep on, other tragedies to uncover, tragedies brought about by a half dozen revolutionaries of the twenty-fifth hour who in a moment of rage unleashed their unadulterated hatred on their fellow Hueans. **

We moved under a crepuscular sky and in the pestilential rain, like an aimless and half-blind swarm of bees after their hive had been totally, irremediably destroyed.

A permanent shroud has fallen on the Imperial City of Hue, the Beloved City of Hue, even though here and there messages of peace and forgiveness still ring on.

* The Blessed Tong Viet Buong was canonized in 1988 along with 116 other Vietnamese martyrs by Pope John-Paul II. He is now called Saint Paul Tong Viet Buong.

** I am not interested in discussing the massacre in Hue. Opinions vary; some said only a few hundreds were killed; others talked about tens of thousands. We can talk to people who lost loved ones during the massacre. We may want

to read Nha Ca's haunting   "Mourning Headband for Hue". We may also maintain that there was no killing in Hue. But then we join the ranks of those who in the same breath affirm that there were no political prisoners in Vietnam after 1975. I was there, in Hue, in the last days of the Second Battle for Hue.

The Village Mayor and the Colonel

Tay Linh together with nine other villages formed the Ten Imperial Villages. Originally, they were diversified. Five of them, including Tay Linh, were to provide the Imperial Court and the Imperial Guards all the food they would need in the case of a long siege by any enemy force. Five others were to provide tools and weapons for the need of the Imperial Citadel under siege. Citizens of the Citadel enjoyed many privileges including the exemption of any postage for their outgoing mail. It was here that every year, in the spring the Emperor would go into the field and plow the first furrow, to open the planting season for the villages and the country. Indeed, the villagers in the Citadel believed they were superior to all the villagers around the country. But unbeknownst to them the old and familiar world was crumbling and they were no longer privileged citizens.

This was what took place in Tay Linh Village one day in April, 1945, not long after the Japanese coup de force of March 9 when the uneasy alliance with the Vichy French ended and the Japanese occupation started for good over all the three former kingdoms of Indochina.

Hue was for a flitting moment the Capital of independent Vietnam again. But the Imperial Court and the Ten Imperial Villages were still under the protection of the Japanese Imperial Army while Mang Ca Fortress was manned by a Japanese Regiment.

In the afternoon, the interpreter, who served in the Japanese Imperial Army hurried back to the village and haltingly told the village mayor that two Vietnamese drifters had somehow succeeded in penetrating the Mang Ca Fortress and were both caught stealing food in the Officers' Mess Hall.

The interpreter was not born in Tay Linh; he was a Northerner who had followed the Japanese Imperial Army on its march southward. For the moment, he lived in a rented room, at Mrs. Dau's home. And the bad mouths of the village scandal mongers had started gossiping about the widow and her renter.

The village mayor was distressed because some of the villagers had also got into the Fortress and stole food from the Japanese. If the drifters got caught, it was highly probable that some of the villagers would soon be caught.

The mayor was rated rather high by the villagers for his management of the village business, because he was honest and perseverant. His approval rate was higher for his work as the chairman of the Parish council because he really cared for the rich and the poor, the saintly and the sinners. For years already, the two functions had always gone to the same person, nobody knew why.

The villagers were ordinary people who were hard-working, honest and good Catholics. But by June 1943 famine had spread from the North to the provinces of Central Vietnam. And at least some starving people knew no law.

Mayor Van sent messengers to all the households and decided to personally visit the more *vulnerable* families, meaning families with young adults who had been known to be less honest and law-abiding than others.

By nine in the evening, words came from the interpreter that the two drifters had been interrogated by the Kempeitai (*Japanese Military Police*) and that a stupid Kempeitai sergeant had unintentionally killed them. The mayor was distraught. He sent out messengers again telling the villagers of the bad news and asking them never to come close to the Fortress walls.

By midnight a squad of Japanese soldiers was sent out of the Fortress. They carried with them spades, storm lanterns and the bodies of the two drifters. Apparently, the Japanese command in the Fortress wanted to bury the bodies in the no man's land between the Fortress wall and the village bamboo hedges.

Traditionally, that no man's land was considered as village land and villagers never failed to plant corn on it year in and year out.

And though there was no such thing as a village gate, anything close enough to the village bamboo hedge facing a southwest corner of the Fortress wall was considered to be part of "the village gate".

*

Sipping tepid tea, the mayor kept asking the witnesses to repeat their reports. He was in trouble, he knew that. He would have to act. Yet every course of action imaginable terrified him. Nobody was allowed to bury a dead man near the gate of the village. The dead thieves would have to be disinterred and reinterred properly in some distant cemetery. And the persons who buried them there would have to be fined severely, even if they happened to be soldiers of the Imperial Japanese Army.

The Japanese soldiers who buried the bodies hastily had committed a crime against the village code that said: "No burial at the Village Gate." Transgressing that clause of the village code was a grievous crime that could not go unpunished according to the Village Code which had for centuries trumped even Imperial edicts.

The problem was: how to punish the Japanese Imperial Army? The Fortress was manned by a whole regiment, commanded by a full Colonel. The village had fewer than 150 adults and only about 40 able-bodied men. The *balance of force* tipped completely on the Japanese side, as they were equipped with the most sophisticated weaponry while the village men were with some stretch of the imagination armed with an assortment of sharp tipped bamboo staffs and machetes. Only two men got swords and one got a revolver.

Mayor Van was not a hero. And he was not an adventurer. He knew it and everybody in the village knew it. All knew that fate had put the mayor in an untenable and desperate situation. Fate was about to ruin him. Fate was about to get him killed. The mayor – who otherwise was a model Christian -- had always believed in Fate more than in God. And now when Fate was about to play the dirtiest trick on him, he could not decently turn to God to ask for help!

But punishing the Japanese Imperial Army for what it had done was an absolute *must*. If for one reason or another, any reason, Tay Linh village failed to levy a penalty on the Japanese occupation troops, every Tay Linh villager, old or young, man or woman, would lose face and would be covered with opprobrium.

On the next morning, the fear of being covered with opprobrium brought more and more villagers to the home of the mayor, asking him to go to the Mang Ca Fortress and deliver to the Japanese Commanding Officer a letter demanding a meeting, in effect, an ultimatum.

The mayor's home was L-shaped. The main structure, facing south, was where the mayor sat. It was there that he conducted village and parish business. The other wing faced west. It was where his farmhands ate their dinners next to the kitchen.

The mayor looked out at the villagers. They did not dare invade the square paved threshing floor. They stood as a noisy crowd around the floor, debating among themselves and suggesting suicidal options to the mayor.

While the mayor procrastinated, the hot headed youths started gathering in small bands elsewhere and arming themselves with knives and machetes. They were ready to assault, they said, the Japanese garrison behind the Fortress walls.

Two large groups of young girls and women also prepared themselves to do battle, armed simply with fighting staffs.

As the information about those bands and groups reached him, the mayor kept saying: "Preposterous! That is absolutely absurd!" But he did not see any solution. The village council members had all come and were now, sitting comfortably around him. They gave him advices on how to approach the Fortress gate *without being shot.* He looked at them, his loyal colleagues in good time but not necessarily in bad time with contempt and resentment. They were about to throw him to the wolves and apparently had no qualms about doing just that.

He called out to his wife to prepare lunch for everybody, notables as well as commoners. His wife, the maids and the village matrons who came with their men, had no problem killing a pig and a few chickens and cooking for over fifty people.

Some men ran home and brought back a few rice wine jugs.

*

While everyone else was enjoying the meal, either sitting in his house, or standing in his yard, the mayor had some difficulty eating his "last meal". He knew there was no escape. *"Noblesse oblige"*, he would have to do what he had to do. *"Noblesse oblige"*, that's what his predecessor told him, even though neither of them spoke much French.

The rice wine was barely drinkable and he knew he should not be inebriated when he faced the armed sentinels of the gate of the Fortress. "I will not die intoxicated," he said to himself. With trembling hand, he stroked his bear and muttered:" I will not be humiliated either."

*

At three in the afternoon, the mayor led a shaken village council to the gate of the Fortress.

When they arrived at a hundred yards from the gate, half a dozen Japanese sentinels charged with their bayoneted rifles. The soldiers stopped short at a couple of steps from the mayor.

A little behind the "delegation", Tay Linh villagers stood stoically. The mayor held out the letter demanding a meeting with the commander of the Fortress. The soldiers looked at the paper but would not touch it. A Japanese sergeant discarded the threatening half circle of soldiers and shouted in

Japanese something that none of the villagers understood. The sergeant had his hand on the handle of his short sword. He rattled his *guntō* against its steel-lined scabbard and looked angrily into the mayor's eyes.

Trembling like a leaf, the mayor responded by shoving the document into the sergeant's face. Another shout from the Japanese startled the mayor, his council and the villagers. But none of them stepped back.

Finally, the Japanese sergeant snatched the paper from the hand of the mayor. The text was written in Chinese ideograms. The sergeant stared at the document a moment until he understood the first line on the right side of the paper: "Respectfully to the Great Commanding Colonel imploring his perusal".

He turned on his heels and walked back to the gate of the Fortress. The Japanese sentinels also retreated to the gate, leaving the mayor, his council and his villagers on the spot. After a long moment, the mayor said: "There is nothing else to do here. Let's go home and wait for *their* answer."

*

At five, the answer came: A battalion of Japanese soldiers in tight formation followed their Colonel, Takeda Sato, who marched nonchalantly in front of them like a conqueror. And indeed, he was. He had only a month earlier assaulted the Fortress at the head of his regiment and it was him who accepted the capitulation of the French commander and his troops.

The Mang Ca Fortress held on against the Japanese longer than any other French outfit in all French Indochina. It held until the sunset of March 10, almost one day after the Japanese coup de force was launched. For that reason, when the French Colonel surrendered his sword to Sato, the latter showed him every sign of courtesy and respect.

The courtesy and respect were well deserved as the French garrison was armed with weapons of World War I vintage and as their rifle-propelled grenades never exploded, having been stored for too long in the Fortress damp ammunition dumps.

Now marching in front of his troops Colonel Sato wondered how he would deal with a mob of unarmed Vietnamese. The tone of the letter to him was respectful enough but the content was most insulting: the little mayor was talking about heavy fines to be levied against the offending Japanese Imperial Army.

To use force against a rebellious village would be normal as Japan was at war. And at war, abnormal actions were frequently judged to be absolutely normal.   But killing civilians in the context of Tay Linh's insolent behavior was out of question: As the commander of the Mang Ca Fortress Colonel Sato was responsible for the security of the whole Citadel and the *ten Imperial villages.* Furthermore, his area of responsibility included the Imperial Palace too. That meant he was responsible for the security of the emperor, and the imperial family, and by extension, all the inhabitants of the ten Imperial villages.

Vietnam was now nominally independent. It had become part and parcel of the Greater East Asia; and therefore the mob of Tay Linh village was part of Greater Japan.

A military man to the core, Sato had now to act like a politician and a diplomat.

But what should he do now with this Tay Linh mob? A bad move here and he would lose his command *at the most*

29

critical moment of Japan's history. Sato was high-ranking enough to know that Japanese defeat was merely a matter of time, a matter of days. And he wanted to fight to the end. He wanted to keep his command until the end.

The old mayor went to the gate of his garden to greet the Japanese. Inside, villagers thronged around his front yard. They were soon pushed back by Japanese soldiers with their rifles and bayonets. They stepped a few steps back, then could be pushed back no further. The Japanese looked fierce but did not try to hurt anybody. So, it was finally a standoff.

Colonel Sato did not seem to see the confrontation. He walked briskly to the open parlor in the mayor's house. The mayor did not like the reversal of the order of host --first, guest, second--, but did not show his annoyance. With a wave of his hand he invited the Colonel to sit down. He sat down facing the Colonel and with a shy smile showed the paper, brushes and inkpots on the table, everything ready for a *written* dialogue; of course, a written dialogue in Chinese calligraphy.

Colonel Sato was a very tall and handsome man. Though he was not in his dress uniform, he did not neglect to put on his gold stripes and his glittering military decorations. His long sword seemed to make a tremendous impression on the villagers. Yet, he knew he was at a disadvantage. He would have to hold a written conversation with this little old man half his size, a peasant. He regretted that he had not seen it fit to follow in the footsteps of his father and learn Chinese calligraphy more assiduously.

The village mayor was frail and walked unsteadily, perhaps due to arthritis. He wore heavy glasses that deformed the shape of his eyes. The eyes kept blinking furiously, showing fear.

The interpreter was apparently allowed to look over their shoulder and read what was being written and report to the Tay Linh crowd and the Japanese soldiers on what was being said.

The village mayor opened up by writing:" I am most honored to welcome you to my humble abode. I humbly ask the Colonel to transmit my greetings and best wishes to his Majesty the Emperor of the Greater Japan."

The Colonel didn't know what else to do but to bow deeply to thank the little village mayor for his wishes. Then, throwing his shoulders back he wrote quickly: "You are showing disrespect to the Imperial Army. For that, the punishment is death. Are the villagers rebelling against the Imperial Army? For that, the punishment is painful death."

The interpreter shouted the questions and the answers. The villagers shouted back: "We'd rather die than be humiliated."

Colonel Sato stood up. The villagers shouted once more: "We'd rather die than be humiliated." Now Sato was sure that the villagers and the little mayor had a clear disadvantage. "Force counts for nothing when your opponent shows no fear of death", said his father.

The Colonel listened to the interpreter. His face showed anger, then dawning comprehension. He looked down at the trembling mayor then looked into the crowd again.

He sat down and read the answers of the little man:" We honor the Imperial Army and we are loyal to our Emperor who has urged us to cooperate with the Imperial Army, so rebellion is out of the question."

The Colonel looked at the little man again: he was in every way different than his father. But for a second Colonel Sato saw the same pride, the same moral if not physical courage in both of them.

He penned carefully: "So, what do you want from us?"

The mayor answered with a flourish: "According to our village code, the person or persons who buried the bodies at out village gate must pay a fine."

Colonel Sato asked: "Do you mean you want the Imperial Army to pay a fine?"

The mayor wrote: "No, our village code does not mention *The Imperial Army*, it says person or persons."

He poured tea for the Colonel, and Sato in turn, poured tea for the little man. They sat in silence for a long while sipping tea.

Sato sighed and wrote the dreaded question: "What is the amount of the fine? "

The mayor wrote: "For burying a body at the village gate, the fine is five buffaloes; for two bodies, the fine will be ten buffaloes."

For all answer, Colonel just stared at the little man until the latter took his brush again and added: "Because the person or persons who committed the offense are related one way or another to the Imperial Army, and as we in this village are under the protection of the Imperial Army we are ready to reduce the fine to five buffaloes."

Colonel Sato burst out laughing then using a gesture that everyone understood, he raised two fingers in the air.

Not to be left in the lurch, the mayor raised and waved three fingers. And the haggling stopped there. The Colonel turned to the interpreter and asked him to translate: "Tonight my men will unbury the two bodies and moved them to a suitable place. Ask the mayor where should I go and get three buffaloes?"

The mayor shook his head: "I don't know Colonel" he said through the interpreter. The Colonel laughed again then said, also through the interpreter: "You will get your three buffaloes tomorrow morning."

On that, Colonel Sato headed out of the mayor's home, marched across his front yard and exited by the gate, followed by his sizable escort. The Colonel was more than amused by the incident. He would like to know what the little mayor would do the next day when the payment of the fine would be made, *to the letter.*

*

The mayor was distraught. The more closely he looked at the three buffaloes the more disturbed he was. He called out to the chief of the western hamlet asked him to come to him then asked: "Do you recognize these buffaloes." The hamlet chief was half-blind. He strained his eyes looking for the nicks on the buffaloes' ears, and giving light taps on their necks. Then to the amazement of everyone, he threw himself on the paved rice threshing area of the mayor's front yard and rolled over and over laughing until he lost his breath.

The mayor asked, fearing the truth: "Why do you laugh?" The hamlet chief cried out finally: "You got three buffaloes that belong to the Tay Loc village's mayor." *(Tay Loc was the village to the west of Tay Linh).*

The roaring laughter that came from the crowd who had come and watched jubilantly the ceremonious payment of the fine, was irrepressible. When it died down, the mayor shouted: "We have been outsmarted by the Japanese! How come you laugh when you all should be crying?"

No matter, since that day whenever a villager saw the mayor, he would raise three fingers in the air and laugh.

*

This is not a funny story though.

A couple of months later, Japan surrendered to the Allies. Every day at sunset we saw the Japanese line themselves up on top of the thick wall of the Fortress against the darkening sky and sing. Whatever they sang to the setting sun, the songs seemed to say: "Japan had lost the war." And here in a distant land, undefeated soldiers were saying goodbye to their country's dream of grandeur and conquest, as they tried to reconcile themselves with becoming prisoners of war.

Villagers would come close to the foot of the wall and watch the tears on the tanned faces of the Japanese soldiers. Every day, they ended up crying with the soldiers whom they had learnt to hate.

Standing in the middle of the line of singing soldiers, every day, Colonel Sato cut a proud and tragic figure against the sky. Every day, he saluted the villagers when the singing ended and before he gave the order to his troops to disappear behind the dark wall of the Fortress.

*

A few days before the Chinese troops, part of the Allied Forces, were to see him surrendering his sword to them,

34

Colonel Takeda Sato, in front of his regiment, calmly performed the rituals of seppuku with his short blade. Though his suicide was not witnessed by any villager, we got all the detail of the rituals through the interpreter.

Colonel Sato's body was buried inside the Fortress wall, near the gate of our village. No one told the "victorious" Chinese of his whereabouts. Not his soldiers. Not the villagers. No way, not the villagers.

Sunset Lights

Stressa Hamilton met Rahiji Abaza in 1998 in Alexandria, in Egypt, and got married to him in 2000. In 2002 their daughter Rehema was born in Beirut, Lebanon. In 2004 they moved to Alexandria, Md. as Rahiji had been appointed as counselor at the Egyptian Embassy in Washington DC. In 2007, Rahiji joined one of the most virulent groups in the Muslim Brotherhood network. In August 2008 his daughter Rehema was killed in a car accident. There were some indications that she actually committed suicide after a stormy argument with her father. Rahiji and his group were killed in an explosion in New York in 2009. Documents show the above to be facts. But are they?

"While you were young you lived in the world of action; now, with age, you enter the world of deep feelings." He muttered as if to himself. I looked up and saw his wrinkled face and his tired eyes. He had never been much of a philosopher and what he said did not matter much to me. What mattered was his continued presence among us, the living proof that our genes would carry us through a very long trajectory on the axis of time, that longevity was our privilege and that none of us, except by accident, would die before the age of ninety.

But Dad wouldn't let go of his train of thought. He said: "When you were young you were too preoccupied with the rush of hormones to notice that you were building up stone by stone, minute by minute, a lofty esplanade, from where you would one day contemplate your life in a panorama." What did he say? White clouds tinged with red sailed by over our heads.

Soon enough the friars in the monastery built on the cliff projected far into the lake below would ring the Angelus, three strokes, three strokes, three strokes, then nine strokes, while the sun sunk down behind the western hills.

He had never raised his voice since he sensed that we stopped listening to him. He had learned to say things more to himself than for our benefit. Yet we knew that without his voice in the background, those moments we spent with him would be far less meaningful, far less reassuring.

This time I left Virginia and went back to see him when I was mentally and physically devastated and my life and my heart were in tatters. His tired eyes took me in, made me at home and promised me healing (what healing could I look for when Rehema, our only child had left the world and my husband of twenty years had sued for divorce?).

We were sitting on the raised deck behind my Dad's house, penetrated by the strong fragrance of frangipani blossoms and myriads of tiny Asian jasmine stars. I told him, not really hoping that he would understand me:" Dad, Rehema died three months ago." He nodded as if he understood. He looked into my eyes a long time before he said:" Rehema! Her name means "Compassionate". May God be compassionate to her!" A chill ran up my spine: Rehema had committed suicide and since that day I had distinctly heard the thunderous voice of Allah resonate in the chambers of my tortured mind again and again: *"My slave has caused death on herself, so I forbade Paradise for her."* In my moments of extreme torment I heard the stern condemnation: *"If she kills herself with a dagger, her punishment is to sink the dagger in her heart again and again."*

I was scared for a moment, because apparently my Dad not only knew that Rehema had committed suicide but had an intimate knowledge of the Sharia, as he apparently referred to it: *"Do not kill yourselves, because Allah is compassionate towards you."*

But again, maybe he spoke without understanding. He took my hands within his gnarled hands though. He said: "I know for certain that if Rehema has committed suicide she still is in Heaven, because our God is The Compassionate God. She learned about God's compassion on my knees, don't you remember?"

My voice was strangled with tears. I insisted: "But she grew up believing in Allah, not in God." He shook his head slowly, as if defeated by my argument. A long moment passed before he said: "For many there is that distinction, but not for our Rehema!"

I pulled my hands out of his hands and threw my arms around his neck and with my head resting on his frail shoulder, I cried and cried, pouring all the bitterness, all my fears and all my despair into him.

After a long while, I felt him sag under the weight of my pain and, straightening up, I looked at him and blurted it out: "For the longest time, we had thought that your mind was gone."

I said "we" though my Mom was no longer with us and my Dad lived with my old aunt, Sarah, who rarely expressed an opinion. Strangely enough, my Mom's presence still pervaded everywhere in Dad's home and garden.

I said "we" because I still wanted to include Mom in every part of my life, even though evoking her gave me pain.

Dad nodded silently then said: "You have to be strong, Stressa. Talk to Gahiji. Talk to him and make him understand that any thing under the sun can be mended. Tell him that as he is now, he represents a terrible danger to himself, if not to many others."

I shook my head: "He will not listen to me, Dad. He is suing for divorce, and he hates me."

He sat motionless, facing the balmy garden. Gusts of the evening breeze stirred the fragrance of garden flowers, mixing it with the strong smell of sand dunes, rocky canyons and limestone. He said: "Search in your heart for the hidden love that you still feel for him, Tressa. Search in your heart for the reasons why you have always loved him."

So, my Dad still was nothing but a foolish dreamer! He did not know that Gahiji, the Hunter, had perhaps been the cause of Rehema's death, and that he had joined the most dangerous terror organization in the world.

I said tiredly: "Yes, Dad." Somehow, I felt betrayed once again.

I got up to go inside. He put his hand on my arm and said softly: "I will see him tomorrow in San Antonio. I called him a few days ago, and he consented to come. Don't you want to see him after I talk with him?"

What he said stunned me and for a moment I froze and couldn't say anything. Then I stuttered: "You summoned him, and he comes?"

Dad smiled shyly, as if he had been caught red handed doing something improper. He nodded and confirmed: " Yes, he will be in San Antonio. And he wants to see you."

I was still in a state of shock. Again, I managed to say: "I don't believe you, Dad. He doesn't trust anybody now. How could he put his life in your hand? And why do you believe that he wants to see me?"

He smiled again, this time with amusement flickering across his tired eyes: "Easy, Tressa, tomorrow you may understand why."

*

The little house on North New Braunsfels Avenue struck me as a safe house as soon as my Dad slowed down and stopped for a minute in front of it.

Safe House! I had known that my father had been in thousands of those like this one. Is he still working for the *Company*?

He looked at me and smiled, saying: "It's right here. But let us park the car a little farther." Another trick of the trade that he had learnt when working for *them?*

When he drove, which was rare now, he acted like a young man with all his reflexes all intact. But from the moment he backed his car into his street this morning, until now, he chose not to say a word. For my part, I was both too bewildered by the adventure and too worried about its outcome that I didn't open my mouth either. Driving from Austin to San Antonio took about an hour but for me the trip lasted an eternity.

Dad parked the car three blocks away and we walked back to the *Safe House*. Before he rang the bell, Dad looked at me a long time and said: " Perhaps we cannot save everything, but if you show your courage something may still be salvaged."

I would want to ask him a thousand questions. But the gate already swung open.

A man who pretended without insistence to be a gardener and a young woman who acted without conviction like a maid seemed to know my Dad quite well. They led us in and pointing to a kind of library asked me to wait there while my Dad followed them into a large room in the back. I heard distinctly the voice of the man: "Mr. Abazza is waiting for you, sir." So, Rahiji was effectively there! My head swam as one minute followed another and I couldn't even think.

Then I heard Gahiji's voice in what seemed to be a heated debate. That did not last very long. Rahiji's voice was lowered to the level of my Dad's. They talked for a full hour. Then my Dad popped his head into the library and said: "He is waiting for you."

*

My face to face encounter with my husband lasted about three minutes. Rahiji looked emaciated but his eyes said that he was at peace with himself. He extended his hand to bid me not to come near him. He said, his voice steady and unemotional: "Sign the papers, Tressa, don't ask me why. Nothing that I do should give you pain. And do not grieve for our daughter. She is safe where she is. "

She is safe where she is? Safe, how? Didn't he and I bury our daughter in the Mount Comfort Cemetery in Alexandria? Didn't we build for her a beautiful marble garden mausoleum? Didn't he and I visited her every day for the first two months? Only when he told me about his wish to divorce me did I come to to visit Rehema all by myself.

My head swam as anger, suspicion, repulsion swirled up in me: "You were there that evening, you had a violent altercation with her, then you did not prevent her from taking your car and drove out blindly into the night. Oh, my God, you killed her. You pushed her to suicide." I heard myself screaming inside. Gahiji only saw my tears, and my muttering: "Rehema is dead, Rahiji; our daughter is dead."

I heard a strangled sound in his throat. He struggled a while then looking straight at me with pleading eyes he repeated: "She is safe, Stressa. She is safe."

He finally turned his back on me. It was only when he was opening the door to get out that I heard him say: "Remember the beach of Alexandria."

Yes, I remember the beach of Alexandria and the marvelous days and nights we spent together at the El-Salamlek Palace Hotel there. It was there that putting the age-old golden ring of his family on my finger, he swore eternal love to me.

I instantly understood that part: no matter what he did, I should never doubt his love for me.

His mentioning the beach of Alexandria meant that he still remembered our mutual vows twenty years earlier and that he still loved me.

I ran to him. Again he extended his hand to bid me not to come any closer. But my love for him surged like a tsunami; I was already in his arms before he could retreat into the hallway. I felt his kisses on my face and my neck, and again on my hair. I went insane with love. I held him so tight that I could feel every one of his heartbeats.

When he succeeded to disengage from me, he looked calmly at me. There was only tenderness and love in his eyes.

There wasn't a trace of reproof for my outburst. He said: "Sign the papers, Tressa, and remember the beach of Alexandria".

With that, he was gone.

*

I stood there stunned beyond words. Then my whole body was wracked by spasms and convulsions. I went down on my knees, then my head hit the floor.

How long did I stay in that position? Five minutes? An hour? An eternity? A shadow came over me. I grabbed my father and screamed: "How could you? Dad, how could you?"

Somehow, I finally understood what had happened. If Rahiji still loved me and he swore on that love that Rehema still lived, then I had to believe him. To believe in him would mean that Rehema accident-suicide was a setup. My inhuman pain made the setup believable to the people Rahiji wanted to mislead. Rahiji and my Dad. Rahiji alone would not be able to pull it off. He had needed a conspirator. And my father was the man Rahiji had always trusted. So, they had brought it off together. And I with my grief perfected the scheme.

I hit my father with both clenched fists and he did not even try to dodge. He did not try to disengage. He waited until my anger subsided and I could say: " So, you have always known that Rehema is still alive! How could you let me suffer for the last three months? Do you know that at times I wanted to kill myself?"

Now he pulled me to him and I slumped with my head on his shoulder. I muttered: " You were in Virginia the night that happened; now I remember. You were there to help Rahiji simulate Rehema's accident-suicide. You were there to gather a badly burned body. You were there to prevent me from having a look at the corpse."

I leant on him and got up. He stood up and gathered me into his arms again. He said: " There is no other way! *They* did not harm or kidnap Rahiji's parents in Cairo. But *they* showed Rahiji how they kept his parents under constant surveillance. Rahiji had to join *them* in order to protect his family. But then, they demanded that he sacrificed Rehema and sued you for divorce to prove his loyalty to their cause. That was how it all started."

Little by little joy seeped back into me. So, Rehema is alive and Rahiji loves me! Waves of happiness surged on and on. I was overwhelmed with happiness.

Then my happiness faded away as I realized that Rahiji still was under the control of *people* who forced him to break our vows. I realized that my husband had been constrained to do that.

I asked my father: " Dad, can you help Rahiji to break away from *them*?"

He shook his head: " No, Stressa. He is in too deeply now."

Trembling with fear, I asked: " Will he have to die?"

My question needed no answer. I knew that he, my beloved husband, my Rahiji, was going to die. Yes, I understood my Rahiji now. I knew that he would have to die to make sure that Rehema, me and his own parents could live in safety.

*

Two months later Rahiji died together with most of the members of his group, apparently while rehearsing a series of coordinated bombings in New York. Apparently, Rahiji or someone in his group somehow triggered the explosion of several bombs the group had built and stored at the site. The survivors of the group who were not at the site were captured a few days later. The group that kept an eye on Rhahiji's parents in Egypt disappeared in one night.

*

I now live in a small village near the Swiss Alps, with my Dad. High up on the cliff of a high mountain was Rehema's Eagle Nest, a fortified castle, defended by two elite platoons of security guards. I no longer look on my Dad as an old man. He and Rahiji have made all of this possible, including the prepayment for Rehema's exorbitant tuition at Eagle Nest and our rustic mansion in P, and the home for Rahiji's parents in Costa Rica.

In the winter we do some cross-country skiing, sometimes with Rehema. I dread and exult whenever Rehema leaves her fortified school and joins us for a few precious days. I am mesmerized each time I look at her face and find her dark eyes. They look exactly like Rahiji's.

This is my world. It is completely separated and disconnected from the world I knew before. But no matter! Here I can from time to time hold Rehema in my arms and have all the time to think about Rahiji and pray for his soul.

My love for him keeps growing.

Andre Nguyen Van Chau

Looking for Mireille

Martin could not sleep all night. He got up early in the morning and made coffee for himself. Jack would get up much later. His company was flexible with working hours; so John would go to work at ten A.M. and leave his office at seven P.M. Jack said, that way he avoided rush hour traffic.

Jack was a good son. He was always quiet, gentle and persevering. He had never left unfinished anything that he had undertaken.

Though Martin had many kids he preferred to stay with John, his youngest. Only recently he started thinking that maybe by staying with Jack he reduced the chance of Jack's ever getting married. So with a sigh, he made a silent vow to leave Jack and go to a nursing home in the near future.

But there was something he had to do first.

He would first go back to Vietnam and look for Mireille. He would go and find her. Oh, he knew fairly well that he might never find her. He might even die on the long trip *home.* But he had to try.

*

Over the telephone the Vietnamese young lady, Lily Pham, had told him she would be at her office of Vietnam Tours at nine A.M. But when he arrived at her office, it was still with the signed "Closed" on the door. It did not matter. He

46

would take a stroll in the mall where Vietnam Tours was located while waiting for her.

He said to himself: "I have to steel myself for the trip, mentally and physically. I've gotten to do more exercise."

He looked into a department store glass window and saw his reflection in it. It showed a frail eighty-eight year old man, who could not stand straight up, because a shell fragment had lodged itself in his neck twenty-five years earlier, in the last days of the Vietnam War. The shrapnel was stuck in his lower cervical vertebrae and no surgeon had tried to pull it out.

He remembered how bad it was when an artillery shell penetrated the thatched-roofed house of his nephew and exploded killing the latter and wounding him. It was the second day after the civilians in Hue received the order of evacuation from the local administration.

A thundering and disorderly stream of evacuees poured southward past stalled trucks, abandoned jeeps and motorbikes on the only highway between Hue and Danang.

With a handkerchief soaked with blood pressed against the back of his neck he had run then walked then run again, blindly. His wife, Martha, and the kids had been sent out of Hue the day before. He hoped that they were safe in his brother's home in Danang.

Battalions and regiments of North Vietnamese troops were pouring into Quang Tri and Hue. Martin knew that if Hue was to fall Danang would not hold either. Would he flee further south? For what purpose? Soon enough, further south, Qui Nhon, then Tuy Hoa, Nha Trang and Cam Ranh would also fall. Ultimately Saigon would fall. So, why should he flee southward?

But he thought: "I should go to Saigon and see my oldest sons before we all end up in a concentration camp."

So he kept running in the rain, trying not to see nightmarish spectacle around him. Yet, half blind as he was, he could see personal tragedies unfolding all around him: a little girl screaming by the roadside, having been separated from her parents, an old woman falling and being trampled upon by the insensate crowd before someone stopped to help her get up, a old man dragging his feet unassisted on the highway with a chest wound...

The nightmarish spectacle around him was nothing compared with the nightmare in his mind when he imagined his children and himself being handcuffed and taken to concentration camps.

He did not know that his eldest daughter had put him and all the members of his family on an evacuation list ensuring their departure for the United States. His troubled mind remembered vaguely that she worked for the American Consulate General in Danang. He didn't know that ultimately, his and Mireille's daughter would step out and take him and his family to safety.

*

Martin now remembered arriving in Saigon. He remembered how, responding to the doorbell, his eldest son opened the door then stood petrified. He had heard reports that Martin had died in a shelling attack in Hue. Other reports had said that Martin had died on the Hai Van Pass near Danang having lost all his blood due to a gaping neck wound.

The joy to see his oldest sons was immense. His oldest daughter soon assured him that all of the family would soon been taken to Tan Son Nhat airport and flown out of the country. Anthony, his eldest son did not want to leave with the family. He said he had friends and students he might be able to get out of the country at the end.

Anthony was adventurous, had always been. Martin hoped that the army of guardian angels who had been busy keeping him alive so far would find a way to take him to safety this time too.

*

No, he did not want to remember what happened next in Saigon: the pointless exams at the Grall Hospital – pointless because the French doctors refused to extract the shrapnel from his neck--, the assembly point at night, the short bus trip to Tan San Nhat Airport, then the flight to Guam –, then the flight to Fort Chaffee refugee camp joining over forty thousand other refugees already there.

Leaving Saigon in the chaos and arriving in Fort Chaffee without Anthony, Martin had problems adjusting to camp life, lining up for hours to get some white rice doused with fish sauce. He kept asking around for Anthony, until one day he found the latter at the door of his building inquiring about him.

Martin hid his tears of joy when Anthony told him that he flew out of Tan Son Nhat on one of the two last planes that took off before the runways were shelled and rendered unusable. So once again the angels had not deserted him.

*

Now strolling in the half-awakened mall he did not want to remember the first job in New Orleans where his family was first resettled, then other jobs, then retirement. He did not want to remember cities he had visited or lived in, the lakes and rivers where he had fished or crabbed.

He did not want to remember how and when he had become a permanent resident with a green card, how and when he had become a US citizen.

What he wanted to focus on at the moment was Mireille's face: the dimples on her cheeks when she smiled, her fears, her worries, her sadness, her pain. He said:" I am going to go back to Vietnam. I will go looking for you, Mireille. Help me find you."

Yet whenever he tried to focus on Mireille, another face appeared in his mind, that of Martha, his second wife. He lived with Mireille nine years before she died. He lived with Martha for fifty years.

Now that both of them were gone, their voices, their words, their special ways of doing things blended together and became undistinguishable. They were second cousins anyway!

*

He stopped, turned on his heels and went back to the Vietnam Tours office. When he said his name Lily Pham apologized profusely: "I had to drive my son to school. The traffic was terrible."

Martin thought: "My parents never drove me to school. As a matter of fact, nobody owned a car in my village. Not until 1955, when I was already forty-four year old. None of my children got a ride to school either. Sure, now my great-grandchildren got a ride to school on a school bus or in their parent's car every school day. I am now eighty-eight year old; so over the last forty-four years things have changed quite a bit. No, the changes that had taken place took a seventeenth-century Vietnam and turned it into a twenty-first-century country; and he had in his lifetime gone through four centuries.

He remembered that he did buy a bicycle in 1947. He was the first in the village to own such a wonder. He was also the first in his village to build a brick house two years later.

Lily Pham said: "If you pay cash we will give you a discount." He nodded: "Yes, I will pay cash." He thought:" I have a checking account, but no credit card. Few Vietnamese refugees my age hold a credit card. We still live in a cash base community. The younger generations, of course, will hold credit cards; they will buy homes and cars on credit. Living on credit will be their way to get Americanized."

Lily Pham tried to sell him term-life insurance, a stopover in Hong Kong, an excursion into Cambodia to see Angkor Wat and Angkor Thom. But he doggedly repeated: "I just want a roundtrip ticket: Phoenix to Saigon and back."

A well-dressed elderly Vietnamese walked into the office. He was about to say something to Lily when he recognized Martin. He exclaimed: "My God, here you are, Sir! Where do you need to go? Lily, this gentleman was my boss in Vietnam, he is also my benefactor. Take good care of him."

Martin greeted the man politely: "How are you, Mr. Liem."

Apparently he was the regional sales manager of Vietnam Tours. Lily, on her feet as soon as the man walked into her office said tamely: "Yes, Sir, I am taking good care of him, naturally, Sir. He just wants a roundtrip ticket to Vietnam."

Whatever was the reason for her boss to come into her office seemed to have evaporated because he touched the brim of his hat and was gone.

Lily Pham looked somewhat relieved by his exit.

She became solicitous: "Sir, I will take care of the visa. The service is included in the bill." She looked at him and asked:" Are you going to Viet Nam by yourself?" He nodded. She shook her head: "It will be a long trip, Sir; maybe you will need some family member to accompany you."

He shook his head vigorously: "No, I want to travel by myself."

She said: "You declared here that you would visit Hue and Thanh Hoa, though you didn't book any flight for those trips. I assure you that traveling by train or by bus will be back-breaking."

Martin did not hear her. His mind followed two different tracks at the same time. On one hand, now that Liem had seen him buy tickets to Vietnam, the gossip would start in the Vietnamese community in Phoenix. Someone would soon ask Martin's children about his trip.

Martin did not want his children to know too far in advance of his planned trip: They would try to accompany him on this trip. Horror! This is the only time in his life when nobody would interfere with his plans and his wishes!

He thought: "I may have to rebuke them most brutally if they offer to accompany me."

He muttered: "None of them will be able to derail my plans."

On the other hand, his mind also was diverted to Liem's irruption into the Vietnam Tours office.

While serving as one of Martin's assistants, Liem had already had the reputation of a lady man. Martin had once warned Liem that there were rumors about his harassment of his female staff.

It was a long time ago. He had all but forgotten about Liem. But now little things about the past seemed to come back easily to haunt him. No, he shouldn't be sidetracked like that.

He said to himself: "I have to remain focused. I am going to look for Mireille. I have to focus on that."

*

Lily Pham told him: "When you arrive in Saigon, you will have to go through customs and airport police. Some people have told me that customs officers expect a tip. If you don't pay the tip, they will open everything in your suitcases."

Martin said:" I will carry a small suitcase, they can look as much as they want."

She said: "Airport policemen also expect a tip too. Usually people put a twenty-dollar bill folded in the passport."

Martin shook his head and said: "I have never taken or offered a bribe. I am not going to start doing that now."

He said that firmly while he was totally unsure of what he would do. Some people told him that a small bribe would save him of lots of unpleasant scrutiny. But others pointed out that if he paid the bribe *they* might denounce him for attempting to bribe an officer and drag him to court.

He looked up and talked to Mireille: "Everything is complicated these days. It is a good thing, maybe, that you did not live on to see all these changes."

*

The plane landed at Tan Son Nhat airport very early in the morning. The arrival building was almost deserted until the passengers of his own flight came in.

The lights were bright. On the walls, red and yellow banners proclaimed that an anti-corruption campaign had been launched. Other banners more discreetly warned that no bribing was permitted.

The old airport policeman looked at Martin, and then looked at his passport then asked: "Tourism or visiting relatives?"

Martin said: "Tourism." Was it a wrong answer? Lily Pham had warned him that if he said "tourism" *they* would object, because *they* wanted the "tourists" to come to Vietnam only in special tours organized by pre-approved tourism agencies.

He could say: "Sorry, I mean, visiting relatives." But then *they* would ask him to provide them the list of relatives he wanted to visit! And he did not think that giving the list of his relatives to the police was a good idea.

The old policeman behind the glass window looked at him intensely for a few seconds, and with a sigh he stamped Martin's passport, and turning to a young policeman, apparently his assistant, he said:" Go help him with his luggage. Don't you see that he is eight-eight years old?"

Though Martin only carried a small suitcase, he simply said" Thank you very much", when the young policeman took it from his hand.

So his fears were for naught? Seeing his name on the passport *they* could have asked him whether he was a deputy province chief in the 50's and 60's. But they didn't.

He thought: "They didn't even ask me for a bribe before they stamped my passport".

Outside the building, the young policeman said: "There are plenty of cabs here, but you have to be careful. Some of the drivers are robbers. Here is a cab you can take with confidence. It is owned by a reputable cab company".

The first contact with the *authorities* was not bad, he had to admit. But he knew that he should not relax. Many of his former colleagues and their children still were in reeducation camps. Many of his relatives had died in those camps. Many had been released but unable to find employment because of what they had been before *reunification.*

He said to himself: "I have to stay focused. I have come back here to look for Mireille. Nothing else matters."

*

Martin asked the cab driver to take him to a modest hotel in District One, Saigon Center. The driver said: "You don't need to pay too much for a room. I will take you to a hotel with good reputation, and costing only thirty dollars a night."

Martin insisted: "But it needs to be located near the center of the city. I want to be able to walk to a restaurant, the Central Market and the main avenues."

55

"The driver said:" Of course. I understand." Martin suddenly realized that he had no real plan for things to do in Saigon. Over the last months he had wanted to go back to Saigon to confront his friend, Lam. Indeed, Lam, who had once stayed as a house guest for over two years at Martin's home, and who had obtained one job after another thanks to Martin's intervention had *forgotten* to warn him about Thanh Hoa provincial authorities' decision to turn the cemetery where Mireille was buried into residential land. What a shock to Martin when he finally found out far too late about the decision! Yes, he found out about the decision only a few months ago, and he learned at the same time that Lam had gone back to Thanh Hoa and leisurely moved the remains of his own brother out of the cemetery before the announced deadline. The grave of Lam's brother was only a few meters away from Mireille's.

Even now that Lam had died, Martin, remembering the episode, still muttered angrily: "And at the time you went to Thanh Hoa and took care of your brother without a look at Mireille's grave, I was sending you monthly checks to help you and your family. You were a heartless man!"

His anger did not last long. He shook his head and said to himself: "My heart has no more room for anger. I have to be perfectly calm. The search for Mireille's remains will not be easy. I have to have all my faculties with me."

Some sources of the latest information on that matter that Martin obtained from Thanh Hoa indicated that all the remains that had not been reclaimed by relatives were brought into a warehouse belonging to a Catholic parish and that the parish priest conserved them there.

Other alarming sources said that the markings of names and years of death on the temporary coffins in the warehouse were gone or had faded with time.

Some sources said that within a few months, all the unclaimed coffins would be buried in a common grave by the authorities.

Martin shook his head again: He said to himself: "I am trying to keep the hope of finding Mireille. But deep inside me, far deep inside me, I feel that this is too late."

*

He slept for over three hours and woke up at noon. In the early morning, on his way to the hotel he had noticed several small and modest restaurants nearby. He realized though that he was too hungry to walk to any of those eateries. He went downstairs and asked the young day manager whether the hotel can send up some food to his room.

The young manager told him that there was a noodle soup booth in front of the hotel. He said that the noodle soup lady and her grandchild cooked excellent *pho* and that if Martin agreed he could ask her to send up a steaming bowl of noodle soup right way.

Martin looked out of the hotel and saw the old sidewalk vendor and a very young child serving noodle soup to at least a dozen customers who sat at a long table under a tent. Martin shook his head and was about to say no; but he was again conscious that he was really hungry and might not have the strength to walk to a restaurant. He turned to the hotel manager and said: "OK, please have them bring a large bowl of noodle soup to my room. " The manager said: "I can assure you that their *pho* is excellent."

He went up to his room and waited. He opened immediately after the first knock on the door. It was the little girl with a tray, with a large bowl of soup and a plate of soybean shoots, mint and slices of chili and lemon.

She was thin and pale. She did not want to leave after she put the bowl of *pho* and the plate of vegetable and spices on the table. She asked: "Have you come back from overseas?" He looked up at her and nodded. She insisted: "Do you live now in America." He nodded again. She said: "You are a very lucky man!"

Martin was surprised by the intensity of her voice. He asked:" Do you want to go to America?"

She hesitated a long time before she confessed: "Yes, of course."

Again the intensity of her voice startled Martin. He asked: "How do you plan to do that? Unless you have plenty of money, I don't see how you can get to America."

She startled him again when she said: "My grandma and I have been looking for someone who wants to adopt me and take me to America."

This time her voice falters a little. Martin knew that she had seen how flimsy her hope was. Martin said prudently: "Why do you want to go the America? Many Americans are poor and many more are unhappy. Why do you want to go there?"

Something pushed him to squash the desire of the little girl to go and live in America. He said: "Look at me; I worked until I was eighty. But I am poor. I travel with a little suitcase. You have seen many American "backpack tourists", haven't you? I am like one of those. "

She said emphatically: "You are not! I want to be a doctor, like my Dad. He died when I was only one year old. My Mom died two years ago when I was nine. Now I live with

58

my grandma. There is no way for me to go to school and become a doctor like my Dad if I stay here."

Martin asked: "How did your parents die?"

The little girl shook her head, sighed and said: "My father was a military surgeon. He was sent to a re-education camp for twelve years. When he was released he was very sick. He had bone cancer and there was little we could do for him. He died a few years later, when I was one year old. My Mom did not find a teaching position after 1975. She found work from time to time as a bookkeeper. She was broken hearted when my Dad died. She passed away when I was nine."

*

Martin did not mind eating in front of the little girl. From time to time he cast a glance at her, gauging her desire to go to America.

A voice in him- was it Mireille's? - urged him to make a bold and monumental promise: "I will adopt you, little girl." But he knew *that* would be an empty promise. How could he, at his age, take on such a new responsibility? Probably he would die during this trip to Thanh Hoa. Then his promise would be a lie, and the little girl would be broken hearted.

Suddenly, there was a great deal of shouting in the street. The girl ran downstairs, and Martin, opening the window, saw the old lady being screamed at by a corpulent middle-aged man who looked like a typical bully.

Martin left his half-consumed meal and went downstairs. The manager was outside apparently trying to defend the old lady. Martin had lost the use of one ear, so he cocked his head to one side and listened. There was too much screaming and Martin could not make any sense out of what the bully said. But the hotel manager who had tried in vain to stop his screaming came to Martin and said:" Apparently *she* owed him a bunch of money. *She* said that the deadline for the repayment is two years from now; but *he* said he needed the money now and threatened to pull down the tent.

By that time, the customers had finished quickly their bowl of *pho*, stood up, paid the little girl and walked away from the scene, not wanting to be involved. Yet, by then the scene was observed by a crowd of onlookers.

Martin stepped forward and asked: "How much does she owe you?" As soon as the question was uttered Martin was terrified. Why did he take sides? Why did he intervene in something that was none of his business?

The man stepped back and looked at Martin intently. Standing in front of him was a frail old man. Somehow the old man commanded certain respect. The man blurted out: "She owes me ten million."

The amount did not register at first. Martin was horrified by what he was doing. He realized that he had put himself in the center of a melodrama, in spite of his usual reluctance to be part of any melodrama.

Then the amount registered at last. Martin made a mental calculation. Ten million were not a small amount. It represented one tenth of what he brought with him for this trip.

He became a toy of a violent storm that surged in him. He asked the man without thinking: "Do you have papers, receipts for such a debt?"

The man said, a little subdued now: "Of course, I do. Here is the debt acknowledgement letter, duly signed by her."

Martin looked up and the old woman nodded confirmation.

Martin said to the hotel manager: "I will go up to my room and come back with five hundred dollars. That must be enough."

The manager said: "Yes, five hundred dollars would do. But why do you do this, Uncle? You cannot solve problems for everybody!"

Mireille's voice in him became louder: "No Martin, you cannot help everybody but you can help this old woman and this little girl. Isn't that worth doing?"

Strangely enough, he also heard Martha's voice: "She's right Martin, you should help. It's time you start helping people again."

So, both his first and second wife urged him to do something he had already decided to do. He suddenly realized that in a certain way he had become callous and selfish because of his pain after Martha's death and his half-a-century guilt after Mireille died.

Martin hurried back into the hotel, muttering to himself: "I am an old fool; and there is no bigger fool than an old fool."

*

The little girl had replaced the bowl of tepid *pho* with a steaming one. She had also brought up a new plate of fresh vegetables and spices.

The girl asked:" Why did you do that, Sir?"

Andre Nguyen Van Chau

Martin pretended that he did not hear the question and went on working on his bowl of noodle soup.

He thought: "I have spent one-tenth of the money I brought with me, maybe wastefully. I will have to tighten the belt from now on." His thought drifted back to the little girl: "What does she expect from me now? Does she want me to adopt her and take her to America? That would take forever. I am poor. I am going to die soon. No, adoption is out of the question! But I might interest someone to adopt her once I am back in the United States."

The little girl insisted: "Why did you help us, Sir?"

Somehow, all Martin could do was smile. Then all of a sudden he burst out laughing. The little girl looked completely nonplused at his apparently irrational merriment.

She asked again: "Why did you give us so much money? This hotel has never been frequented by wealthy people; therefore, you must be poor. But being poor did not prevent you from giving away what it takes my grandma and me at least a year or two to make."

Martin recovered and said ponderously: "You are right. I am poor. I stay at cheap hotels, eat cheap food, take the train or the bus and watch every dime I spend... But paying your grandma's debt seemed to be the right thing to do; so, I did it. Please, don't mention it again."

The little girl said: "After you paid our debt, my grandma asked me to go up here and plead with you to adopt me or to arrange for me to be adopted by someone you know in America. I thought at first that it was strange to ask you for another big favor after receiving one. But my grandma is right. You are a kind man and you may know other kind people in America."

62

Martin objected: "But how about your grandma? Who will help her after you are gone?"

There were tears in her eyes, but she spoke with a clear voice: "She said she would manage. I have a cousin who lives next doors. He takes us here every day early in the morning and comes here to take us home in the evening on his tricycle; I mean, our pots and pans, our food and our gas tank and gas range. He has a daughter my age. She can help my grandma. Of course, I will miss my grandma and she will miss me."

Martin said: "I am eighty-eight. So, don't count on me to adopt you. I am too old, too weak to raise another kid. I can ask one of my children to adopt you; but all of them have children of their own already. They all work and will not have the time to go through the time-consuming process of adoption. I have a few friends and acquaintances in America, but I would not be able to recommend any one of them to you, because I don't know them well enough. So, you see, I cannot do anything to help you with your wish to go to America."

Martin realized that he was not talking to a little girl of twelve and that the little girl who had experienced so much suffering in her childhood had become mature before her age.

The girl sighed and gave Martin an envelope. He opened it and saw a folded sheet of paper with her name, her birth date and her address on it. There were also a couple of pictures in the envelope. She said: "Grandma knew that you would decline. But she asked me to give this information all the same. She said who knows; maybe you don't see how you can help now; but maybe you can in the future."

Once again, Martin was struck by the contrast between the little girl in front of him and the things she said so naturally.

He said: "I will keep this information. As your grandma said, who knows what tomorrow will bring."

*

Saigon, which in his original plan was of little importance to his trip, had become the scene of an overwhelming drama that Martin could barely understand.

He hoped that the remaining days would not bring him any further surprises. He would like to focus solely on how to look for Mireille.

But human contacts in Saigon had broken the cocoon he had been surrounding himself after Martha passed away. He was now open to more human contacts. Every day, after being served a bowl of *pho* in the morning, he took the bus to go look for all his old friends and acquaintances. He found many who had not moved away from their old addresses. Through them he found dozens of others. All of those men had been released from reeducation centers a while back. He asked them about their years of captivity. But after mentioning the number of years of captivity, after naming a few locations of prisons, they had extremely few stories to tell him.

Apparently they had all tried to forget about the pain and the humiliations of those years. Apparently they had succeeded in erasing even the most salient memories of those years. They never mentioned the cruelties of the wardens, violence they had been subjected to, tortures and beatings. No, when they described their wardens they painted them merely as insensitive bureaucrats who acted like automatons and delivered punishment without exaggerated eagerness. The wardens were seen as unsmiling, humorless, sullen, people who had a job to do and carried out their duties faithfully, no matter the outcomes.

Martin who had expected his friends to talk non-stop about their captivity had to extract from them tiny bits and pieces of their days in hell.

In the end Martin, listening to their silence more than their words, came to see for the first time in his friends real people who were able to endure months and years of pain without complaining, capable of keeping their gaping wounds hidden and of going on with their broken life with relative dignity.

In the evening when he came back to the hotel, he had another bowl of *pho* brought up to his room. He paid for the food and was firm enough to make the little girl know that he would not accept the meals otherwise.

Martin and she never returned to the subject of adoption. But she succeeded in asking for his address and phone number in the United States.

At night, he slept for a couple of hours, and then lay in bed, looking up into the darkness: sometimes Mireille's face with the dimpled smile appeared for a couple of seconds then disappeared.

He found that Mireille seemed to approve his new interest in real people. She seemed happy that he had opened his heart for the first time to his interlocutors and that he no longer tried to judge the merits of his friends and acquaintances.

*

The train was slow. Martin didn't mind. He was onboard the 7:30 AM Reunification train in Saigon. The train would average 40 km per hour; and that meant he would arrive in Hue about 7:30 the next morning. He didn't mind; and as a matter of fact, he enjoyed the long trip ahead.

A friend of his had advised him to take the *Cong An* car where he was surrounded by policemen. His friend said:" That way, no thief would come near you."

Martin found the advice valuable. The policemen let him take a window seat. He knew that from there he could see for hours the coastline of Central Vietnam. He was thrilled with anticipation. The green, turquoise sea that penetrated coves and bays and lapped at shining black rocks and dazzling white sands would bring back memories of his prime youth when he still was a rookie veterinarian sent out on missions to examine and vaccinate the cattle in all the provinces from Thanh Hoa to Phan Thiet, from north to south along the coastline of Central Vietnam.

He had wanted to share the joy of discoveries with Mireille at the time. But Mireille like Martha later on did not like to travel and was only happy in places that were quite familiar to her.

*

Was it a mistake when he accepted the invitation of the little girl, --who now had a name, Mai --; was it a mistake for him to have accepted the invitation to visit Mai's and her grandmother's home? Mai did not have to ask twice. He was curious enough to want to see where and how Mai and her grandmother lived.

They had closed their business early in the afternoon that day, went home and prepared a copious dinner for him.

It was the first time he had a direct conversation with Mai's grandmother. She was many years his junior but appeared to be much older than him. Her wrinkled face, her snarled fingers, blue and back hands, told him her story better than her words.

Neither she nor Mai tried to remind him of his vague promise to help someone to adopt Mai.

It was the night before he was to leave Saigon. At the moment he departed, Martin said: "Please, look for other avenues. I am an old man; I do not know how successful I would be in finding a good couple in America who would want to adopt Mai."

Both the old woman and Mai nodded understanding; but by the way they looked at him, he knew that they counted on him, a lot; no matter what he said.

*

The policemen left him alone. From time to time, when the train stopped at major railway stations, many of them would get down and exchanged information with the local police, or walk around and observe passenger cars and freight cars. Every hour, some of them would walk down the aisles of the passenger cars.

Twice, they brought back two men that they interrogated lengthily but patiently.

Martin did not give them too much attention as he was totally lost in the contemplation of the sea and the beaches.

At noon, during the lunch time, he shared his food with the policemen and they shared with him what food they brought with themselves. Exchanges between him and the policemen were polite but kept to a minimum.

He was grateful to them for not asking him any personal question.

And they seemed to be glad that he did not try to engage them in any serious conversation.

*

At five in the afternoon – half way between Saigon and Hue-- the train arrived in Nha Trang. A couple of overseas Vietnamese- easily spotted as such by his brand shirt and pants and her brand dress – went aboard Martin's car. Apparently nobody had warned them that it was the *Cong An* car. As soon as they recognized the uniforms of the policemen they tried to get out. But it was too late; the train had already started getting out of the station.

They decided to go and sit directly in front of Martin. Yet, because of Martin's crumpled clothes they were not so sure that he also was an overseas Viet. The wife tentatively asked: "Have you been overseas, Sir?" Martin nodded. The husband asked: "From the United States?" Martin nodded again. They introduced themselves politely, but Martin did not retain their names. Their irruption dragged him out of his reverie and forced him back to reality.

A few days earlier he would resent their presence. But the week passed in Saigon had changed him drastically, even if he was not aware of that change as yet.

He apologized and asked the couple to tell him their names again, blaming his impaired hearing. So, Nam and Thu came from Sedona, Arizona. He volunteered this time: "My name is Martin. I know Sedona quite well. Yes, I remember the Indian saying:" The Gods created the Grand Canyon but they stay in Sedona."

Nam and Thu smiled. Nam asked: "Where do you live, Sir?"

"I live with my youngest son in Phoenix", Martin said.

"Oh, we are practically neighbors", Thu said.

Martin thought: "The young always tend to minimize differences and distances; the older people tend to maximize them."

Thu inquired: "So, you are back in Vietnam to visit relatives?"

Martin shook his head: "I only have a few relatives here, most of them distant relatives". He did not know why he avowed: "No, I came back here to look for the remains of my late wife."

Thu and Nam seemed to be electrified. Nam exclaimed: "We are here for the same purpose. The authorities have destroyed the cemetery of Thanh Hoa, and we hope to find the remains of Thu's parents. Are the remains of your late wife being found in Thanh Hoa too?"

Martin said: "It is too much of a coincidence. Yes, I am on my way to Thanh Hoa, with a stop in Hue."

There was a glow on Thu's face, and for a second, she looked really beautiful. Her husband said: "May this coincidence be a good omen for our quest. Until now, we have thought that we were too late."

Martin did not say anything. He suddenly realized that unless there was a miracle, there was no way he could find Mireille's remains now.

*

Martin remembered with vivid colors the coastline of Central Vietnam. It was in one of these provinces that for six years he was a deputy province chief. It was here that a "revolutionary" military junta put Martin in prison. He remembered how that period of time spent in various prisons had taught him to be humble and grateful for every bit of kindness showed him by others.

He remembered how the mother of the "revolutionary" Colonel who put him in prison brought him, in his cell, every day copious meals that she had cooked, and sat outside his cell to talk to him while waiting for him to finish.

He remembered how his *pro bono* lawyer, Anthony's classmate and friend, defended him ferociously against all the false testimonies that the junta had collected for his case. He remembered how a gentle but fearless judge had thrown out all the charges against him.

Now Martin regretted that after he had been cleared of all charges and paid all back salaries, he had become callous and harsh again and forgotten that his strength had always come from his ability to empathize with people and from his respect for others.

He told Nam and Thu about his time in K.H province. He told them about the great pleasure he drew from short visits to villages and his conversations with farmers at the time.

He said: "One day I came to a remote village. The villagers had finished planting cassava before the wet season set in. The district chief, the village mayors and notables were there showing me with pride long rows of cassava sticks freshly planted. I noticed that on each stick planted vertically and protruding just two inches from the ground the planters had

70

thoughtfully placed a flat piece of gravel or stone. They did that to protect the soft core of the cassava sticks, from getting rotten by the rain."

Merriment danced in Martin's eyes as he pursued the anecdote: "I called the villager mayor to come close and told him: "This is cassava traditional planting. You need to change this if you want cassava to have better yield. There was fear in the eyes of the mayor, but I did not care. I said, "Please ask your villagers to plant the cassava sticks obliquely instead of horizontally. You can see by yourself that many more cassava roots can grow out from a stick planted obliquely."

"The village mayor nodded hesitantly. He murmured: "Of course, I can see that." The agricultural chief of the province who accompanied me said: "Then, ask the farmers to do that right away.

"The village mayor paled visibly. He went to talk with the notables. Some of the notables ran to the villagers who stood a little away.

"Some of the villagers ran back to their homes and came back with hoes and spades. And under the direction of the district chief, the agricultural chief and the mayors, they started digging the cassava sticks out and replanted them, this time *obliquely*.

"When I was satisfied that the villagers had bought the new planting technique, I left, with the delegation for another village in the mountain. It was an ethnic village. And as usual, we sat down in the *nha rong* (community house) for the ritual drinking of rice alcohol from a large urn with long stems.

"It took us several hours to sip rice wine with our long stems; and it was almost sundown when we head back to town. But before we descended to the plain, I wanted to have a look at the cassava field of V. village. Triumphantly we walked to the field of cassava and found that all the cassava sticks had been replanted one more time, *vertically.*"

Both Nam and Thu burst out laughing and Martin with them. Thu asked: "What is the moral here, Sir?"

Martin said: "I should have drawn two lessons from that experience."

Nam urged him on: "What are they, Sir?"

Martin smiled vaguely: "First, you cannot change a tradition that easily."

"And?" Thu prompted.

Martin said, closing his eyes: "And second, you should trust the common people much more."

*

Hue was here. The Eternal Hue! He took a room in a small hotel near the Perfume River. He did not want to inconvenience any of his second cousins, grandnephews and grandnieces.

He took a cab to Tay Linh village, where he was born, where he grew up, started a professional career, married Mireille; and later on, seven years after Mireille died, married Martha. It was here that most of his sons and daughters were born.

From the street he could not see his house. He asked the driver to wait and started following a small path to his house. But his house was no longer there. Or rather, his house was surrounded now by four or five other houses which communicated in some way with it. Apparently his house and garden now housed a bunch of high-ranking *occupiers* who did not care for beauty or elegance and whose only concern was to make the cluster of houses grow bigger and bigger so that it could accommodate more high-ranking *occupiers* from the North.

Martin went back to the taxi. But before he got into the car, he had ample time to look at the house where Mireille lived before she was married to him. He looked at the Ngu Ha River. It was a canal more than a river. But during the frequent floods, Ngu Ha River would transform Tay Linh into a muddy lake. The road facing the river was Ngu Ha Street, lined at one time, with two rows of centenary silk cotton trees.

He asked the driver to go around to the back street from where he could see the house where Martha was born and grew up.

Suddenly he found a profound feeling of peace. Martha was Mireille's second cousin and as kids, they had played together, dreamt together; they had gone to the evening prayers and Sunday Mass at the same church, together.

Seeing them together made him happy.

He did not want to see the "reconstructed" Imperial Palace. He did not visit the Imperial Tombs. No, he was not a tourist. He simply wanted to breathe their air of Hue, walk its streets, watch the sunrises and sunsets in Hue, and remember.

He also wanted to see the graves of his parents.

*

Martin stood in front of the graves of his parents in Hue. It rained cats and dogs. His raincoat was not able to prevent cold streams of rainwater from gathering at the base of his neck then cascading along his spine. His grandnephew stood stoically next to him. They did not exchange a word since they came close to the cemetery.

Now Martin had realized that he had two goals when he decided to go back to Vietnam. His obvious objective had been to look for Mireille. But another goal was to see how he himself and Martha would be buried in An Van west of Hue.

For years he had been afraid that cattle that grazed and roamed in the cemetery would one day destroy the graves of his family here. There had been several attempts to solidify the graves, with more or less success. An Van is at a certain altitude, a foothill that rises up towards the Vietnamese Cordillera, that the local people simply call "the Blue Mountains."

So, normally Martin should not be afraid of the graves being flooded in the rainy season. But it was a fact that large hillsides had at times disappeared in a mudslide, when it rained for months in a row, transforming hardened dirt into mud.

He made a mental decision: No matter whether he would find Mireille's remains or not he would have a triple grave here for her, Martha and himself.

But with the demographic growth, with the eternal rain in Hue, how could he be sure that the living would not take over the land of the dead, or that the graves would not be swallowed by a sea of mud.

He had experienced that horror before: One day, he had accompanied his father to the village of Thanh Phuoc, or Tien Non parish, east of Hue, on the bank of the Perfume River. When they arrived, his father, who had never showed emotions, went into shock. The graves of his parents had disappeared. They had disappeared during the most recent flood.

For a long time, his father looked at the river that had gone back to its back and now flowed leisurely. Expressions of anger, devastation, revulsion, resignation followed each other on his ravaged face. Finally, his father turned to him: "What would you say? Vanity, all is vanity? You, who are so proud of your Latin."

Martin said meekly: "Vanitas, *vanitatum, omnia vanitas*, Dad. Vanity of vanities, all is vanity."

His father had looked into his eyes and said: "Remember that, Martin. Nothing endures forever. Nothing in the world lasts forever."

Now on the foothill of An Van, Martin stood in the rain. He mumbled: "Yes, Dad, you are right; nothing in the world lasts forever. But please don't let me stand in Thanh Hoa staring into the void, devastated the way you were in Thanh Phuoc over seventy years ago. Help me find Mireille, please!"

*

It was in An Ninh seminary that Martin learned his Latin. Yes, there were years when he was preparing himself for priesthood. Then, he loved Latin. Few of his classmates could recite from memory long idylls from Virgil's *Eclogues* like him. But some of them ultimately had progressed far beyond his precocious achievements. They had contributed, in a major way, to the history of modern-day Vietnam. He had not.

But from the days in An Ninh seminary, he had acquired a passion for books.

Later on, his reputation was based primarily in his love of books, something he shared with Mireille, who had collected an abundant library for her use.

He continued to read voraciously after Mireille's death, sometimes going through entire libraries from A to Z.

Now he wondered how much good reading had done for him. True, his colleagues were awed by the scope of his knowledge. Some advancement in his professional career was partly due to his scholarship. But there were also adverse consequences. He had become intolerant. And he scared Martha as well as the kids, who never dared challenge his opinions.

He squashed their arguments with a disdainful *non sequitur* or *you need to rethink the issue.*

Now he was eighty-eight and oh, if only he had allowed members of his household to hold on to their opinions and develop their own way of thinking and rely on their own intelligence!

"Regrets will not help", he said to himself.

His steps led him to the *"Acceuil"* library, owned by the Canadian-based Redemptorist Fathers. He had no desire to have another look at the library's book shelves. What he wanted was to look at the structures in Hue that one way or another led him back to the life he had spent there, and opened for him the floodgate of memories, happy and unhappy alike. The Redemptorist Monastery and the "Acceuil" library were among such structures.

*

Lost in his thoughts, he almost collided with a woman. He was about to apologize when the woman screamed: "Oh my God! What you doing here, godfather?"

Her scream startled him. Her calling him "godfather" confused him. He looked at her a long time before he recognized Lai, Martha's goddaughter. He said softly: "Hi, Lai!" She had a baby in her arms and a daughter about eight by her side. He said: "So now you have two children already." She laughed: "No, Godfather, we have five children."

He looked at her again. She was so frail, so thin. She was no more than five feet tall. He exclaimed: "So young, and five children already?" She laughed again: "Godfather, I am thirty years old now."

There were few people walking on the street where they were. From time to time a motorbike or an electric-assist cyclo went past them at high speed.

Lai said: "Would you like to have dinner at our home this evening?"

He was about to decline. But his new self took over and said: "I don't want to be an inconvenience to you, your husband and the kids; but if your invitation is not merely a courtesy, I accept it with pleasure."

Lai said: "Good. Now we have to go to the market. Though we have plenty of caramel pork ribs, and all kinds of cooked vegetables – I usually cook once a day --. But I can do better than serve you reheated food."

She hailed an electric assist cyclo and asked: "Would you mind that the four of us sit in the same cyclo?" He shook his head. "No, if you or the kids don't object."

They went to the An Cuu market nearby. She asked him to take the hand of Sau, the eight-year old girl, and asked the cyclo driver to wait. She went in and bought a small chicken – small compared with the size of chicken in the United States – and a couple of small carps, put all of those in a woven basket that she bought for the purpose and declared: "This will be enough. We have fresh vegetables in our small garden."

She would not let him pay. The second time he tried, she looked at him in such a way that he felt ashamed for it.

Once in her home,-- a small house, but clean and comfortable-- he spent the time playing with her kids, learning their names and making them laugh with stories about America, while she cooked. Long, her husband, arrived home at sundown after she finished cooking.

Martin learned about their relative comfort. Long was a master electrician and earned a good salary and Lai stayed home to take care of the kids.

*

He finally told Lai about Martha's death. Lai looked sad for a moment then looked up and said: "We learned about her passing away a couple of months ago. We believe that she is in Heaven now."

Martin nodded: "She passed away without too much pain. Yes, I believe that she is Paradise now."

At the moment he departed, Martin put five hundred dollars in Lai's hand. She shook her head: "No, Godfather. We have more than we need."

But this time he was firm: "Take it, young lady. Not for you, not for your husband, but for the case where one of your

78

kids needs it. Your Godmother joins me in asking you to take it."

With tears in her eyes she turned to her husband: "You take this money, change it in Vietnam currency and deposit the amount in the bank tomorrow, for our kids."

*

Martin said to himself: "I have started his itinerary with no goal for Saigon, almost no goal for Hue, yet in both places I have experienced life-changing events. What is waiting for me in Thanh Hoa?"

On the train to Thanh Hoa he tried to focus again on Mireille. He couldn't. He was thinking about Nam and Thu. "Have they found the remains of Thu's parents? Would Thu be devastated when her quest ended in failure? Or is she resigned to the fact that her quest and mine are undertaken when it's too late? "

Martin looked at the address they gave him on the train when they approached Hue. He thought: "It must be the address of a five-star hotel." He smiled and said to himself: "There is no five-star hotel in Thanh Hoa, unfortunately for them. I will come there and look for them. But maybe they have already left."

He realized that he had not asked them whether they were working or had retired. If they had retired, it would mean, they had taken early retirement, as both of them looked like they were in the early sixties. The fact that they lived in Sedona pointed to their material wealth.

He had not asked for their address in Sedona. Had he hoped that a fortuitous encounter remained a fortuitous encounter? No, he had hoped to know them better.

He said to himself: "You continue to be superficially interested in other people. Will you change? Will you ask more questions, communicate at another level? Will you try to see other people in three-D? Oh, Catherine, had I squandered the ten years I spent with you, by abstaining from trying to understand your aspirations and your dreams?"

He turned against himself furiously: "And, Martha, I spent fifty years with you and not once had I inquired about your dreams, your hurts and your sufferings. Why was I so insensitive?"

Martin knew that he was exaggerating his past insensitiveness. But he found that something was burning him from the inside. He felt vaguely that he was about to confront the consequences of his past behavior.

The trained went past Quang Tri, then Dong Ha. He looked westward. Yes, the mountains came closer, and Highway 9 cut a swath in the dense forest. Highway 9 led to Khe Sanh, Lao Bao and the Lao-Viet border. He knew the Highway well, even at the time when it was an unpaved red dirt road. He lived in Khe Sanh with Mireille and two-year-old Anthony in a paradise he would never find again. He was young and vibrant. He was the head of the border observation station controlling the cattle trade between Laos and Vietnam.

The landscape behind his office and residence was gorgeous. The streams were teeming with fish and the woods were full of deer and wild hogs.

He was a young man that everybody respected, including the powerful and tough French plantation owners and including the *sub-prefect* (district chief under the emperors). Cattle traders who stopped at his station called him "the great gentleman". To reinforce that notion, the Vietnamese authorities assigned to him a soldier who served as his adjutant.

And yet, even then, he had developed a frantic desire to roam the country. He volunteered for missions that took him as far north as Thanh Hoa, and as far south as Phan Rang, Phan Thiet. He complained that he could only travel in the winter, because for the rest of the year he had to stay at his station to make sure that no sick cattle herds from Laos could cross the border into Vietnam.

That *wanderlust* was satisfied only when he was assigned to work for good in Thanh Hoa a few years later. Missions after missions took him away from Mireille, many weeks at a time. He was happy to be where a cattle epidemic was declared. He was happy to work with cattle herders and owners. He felt great joy to watch a healthy herd graze in some remote district.

Was he selfish to live away from his family half of the time? He wanted to know now.

*

But here the train stopped at Vinh station. It was dark, and it rained hard. He could not see much beyond the yellow lights around the station.

It rained hard that day too in Vinh. The sight of the angry River Ca should have scared them. But the three of them were young. They challenged each other to jump into the river and swim across it. Once they were in the thundering water they knew that they had presumed too much on their swimming skill and their strength. But it was too late.

The river water swirled around them, dragged their feet and thrashed their bodies, all the while driving them downstream toward the sea.

81

Luat, the youngest and who was about to get married panicked first. His screams could be heard for miles. Martin swam toward him, still laughing even though he too was scared. Phan struggled valiantly but had only enough energy to take care of himself. It was up to Martin now to save Luat; he was aware of that. So he swam toward Luat praying that the latter would not go under right away.

The distance between Martin and Luc became greater and greater even though Martin was swimming as fast as he could. Then all of a sudden large dead branches swept past Martin in the rushing water. Martin shouted: "Careful, Luat!"

Luc raised his head above the water, saw the first branch and ducked. He came up for air when another branch hit him in the back of his neck. Maybe the first branch did not kill him, but other branches were already upon him. Martin screamed and plunged toward his friend. But before he could reach Luat, the latter had disappeared underwater.

The rain stopped. The water seemed to get calmer by enchantment. Martin and Phan, and a few people who witnessed what was going on kept diving about, again and again in the turbid water, hoping to find the drowned young man.

Only in the morning of the next day, Luat's body was found a mile away downstream.

A tent was set up hastily by the city authorities on the river bank. Martin and Luc stood guards on either side of a rough open coffin. It rained again all day. In the evening Thanh Tam, Luc's fiancée arrived. She nodded to Martin and Luc then knelt down. Her arms surrounded the head of the coffin. She did not cry. But her eyes were two dark pools of inhuman sorrow.

Only then Martin understood the immensity of the tragedy he and Phan had triggered. He wished he had the power to turn himself into stone. But he was no stone and his body vacillated. He wished he could kneel down next to Thanh Tam. But that would be blasphemy.

His vision became blurred, but looking inward, he saw clearly the flames of Hell.

*

It was almost sixty years ago, but the wound still bled. He wanted to scream, but no sound came out of his throat.

That event, that tragedy had followed him every day of his life. The horror he felt that night would become the source of most of his nightmares.

His guilty conscience had made him later on put his friends above his family, made him care for them far more than he did for his own children. Finding finally the reason for the sacrifices he made in favor of friends over many decades did not bring him relief.

He muttered incoherently: "Stop raining, please stop raining."

*

Martin thanked and tipped the cab driver who had carried his small suitcase into the lobby of the *Thanh Hoa Hotel*. Nam and Thu were supposed to be here at least initially. They might have left.

Only after having booked a room Martin asked the manager whether Mr. and Mrs. Nam were still guests at the hotel. "Yes, they have been here four nights already and don't seem to be leaving soon", the manager said, then he added: "But here they are!"

Nam and Thu came out of the elevator and ran to Martin. Nam said: "We have been waiting for you."

Martin remarked: "You don't look very happy. Must I conclude that the search for the remains of Mrs. Nam's parents has not been unsuccessful so far?"

Tears welled in Thu's eyes. She said: "There still is a tiny bit of hope."

Nam took her hand and said:" Not really. But we will talk about all that later. May I help you with your suitcase? "

Martin shook his head. He said: "I will need to take a nap. Maybe we can have lunch together at noon. In the afternoon, I will go and see the priest who is in charge of the unclaimed coffins."

Nam and Thu exchanged glances and Thu was about to say something but hesitated then clammed up. Nam said: "All right then. Let us be here in the lobby at noon, then go out and have lunch.

*

Martin was so exhausted that he slept all the same, even though from the way Nam and Thu acted, he knew that his hope to find Mireille was no longer realistic. He woke up just in time to brush his teeth, shave, take a shower, get dressed and go down to the lobby.

There was a restaurant nearby – supposedly good --; so they walked the distance. As soon as they sat down at a table Thu said: "May we come with you to see the priest?" Martin smiled: "I don't see why not. But haven't you seen him already?"

Thu said: "Yes, we did see him three days ago. We learned from him that the process went smoothly at first. Lots of people came in time, that is, before the deadline decreed by the authorities. They exhumed the bodies or remains and moved them to another cemetery up in the mountains. On the deadline, the authorities dug up the graves, unearthed the remains and put them in small earthenware caskets (*tieu*). The remains of Catholics were sent to the priest while Buddhist remains were sent to a pagoda, and a large number of remains of ancestor worshippers were sent to a communal house of a village nearby. For Catholics, more than two thousand caskets have been claimed by relatives. But about a thousand of unclaimed caskets are still under the priest's care. He has placed them in a warehouse. The problem is: all the identification labels with name, date of birth and date of death on the caskets are gone."

With a sinking feeling in his stomach Martin asked:" How? How are they gone?"

Nam explained while Thu shook her head then started crying: "The kind-hearted but impractical priest entered in his book all the detail of each casket; then he glued handwritten paper identification labels on the caskets. After a few months, with humidity, cold and heat, with some rainstorms and big winds all the labels were gone. The caskets were no longer identifiable since about eight months ago."

Martin asked: "Would it be possible to identify the remains with a large-scale DNA analysis program?"

Nam shook his head: "We immediately addressed that question to the local authorities. Some other people had asked the same question before. In the United States, DNA analysis, costly as it could be, may be feasible; but not here in Vietnam. And even in the United States such a massive analysis program would take months or years. The authorities are adamant: The unclaimed caskets of Catholics as well as those of Buddhists and ancestor worshippers will have to be reburied next month in a common grave. "

*

Martin said: "I had to see this!" He did not know the limits of his endurance. At the sight of rows after rows of unlabelled caskets, he felt dizzy. He looked at Nam and Thu. The scene was far worse than what they had described to him.

The caskets were set on heavy wooden shelves. They were stacked up three or four in a pile. Many caskets were broken with the remains scattered on the floor.

Nam explained: "Every now and then, some hot-headed and disappointed relatives would throw down the shelves or just used a two-by-four piece of lumber and smashed the unbroken caskets. The parishioners and the priest tried to put back the remains into new caskets, but by doing so they mixed the bones of a broken casket with those of another. Yes, the only option here is a common grave."

The priest came finally. He was defensive. But Martin as well as Nam and Thu did not have the heart to blame him for gluing the paper labels on the caskets.

They shook hands with him. Thu said: "Again, thank you, Father, for what you have attempted to do."

It was then that Martin fainted. Nam and the priest took him to the rectory, where he recovered after a while. He sat up, apologized and suddenly burst into tears. He could not stop the tears. He could not stop the sobbing or the incoherent and strangled words he uttered.

Oh, he had foreseen worse scenarios. But he had not foreseen the limitless devastation he felt now.

After a while he calmed down but again and again he muttered: "Mireille, forgive me." It was Thu who helped him in the end. She started sobbing violently, and Martin, distracted from his own sorrow put a hand on her shoulder and said: "Let's go home."

*

Back in the hotel, Thu said: "We had prayed so much, so hard for a miracle that we came to believe that we would succeed in our quest, no matter what. Then we had found out that we had prayed in vain. After our first visit to the priest we were devastated. Then we heard of a woman, a medium, who could help people identify the remains of their loved ones."

Martin looked at her a long time. She blushed and admitted: "Yes, we knew that going to her for help was wrong. We are Christians and Christians don't use mediums! But we were desperate and we heard repeatedly that the woman had actually been able to help."

Nam sighed and said: "We have tried to see her for all day, yesterday. She has set up a tent in front of her house and the tent has become a kind of waiting room. People who need her help come and sit under the tent until she calls them in. Yesterday, we spent hours waiting, but she never called us. We only left when in the evening one of her assistants came out and told us to leave. She also said we could come back another day."

Martin asked: "Are you going back and try to see her?"

Thu said firmly: "My husband will not go back, but I will. I will go back there, tomorrow."

Martin thought: "Do I witness here a spat between husband and wife?" He said: "Why don't we all go there together tomorrow?"

Both Thu and Nam looked at him with gratitude in their eyes.

Nam said: "Let's ask the manager if he know any good restaurant around town or even on the Sam Son Beach. Martin, you didn't eat anything at lunch."

Martin suggested: "For tonight, I propose that we go to Sam Son Beach. There must be some decent seafood restaurant on or near the beach. But for tomorrow let me ask the manager where we can find real Thanh Hoa home-made cuisine."

What Martin had in mind appeared to be extremely hard to come by. He wanted boiled water spinach, Nghe An salted eggplants (specifying that the eggplants must look translucent), caramelized bacon, and steamed carp. Nam laughed: "I don't believe it!" Thu looked intently at Martin and said: "One of those meals Mireille served you sixty years ago, right."

The manager introduced to the trio his assistant and said: "Maybe Minh can help you. His mother cooks for her boarders."

Minh said: "A menu like this? You will never find it in any restaurant. But it presents no problem for my Mom. Do you want it for tomorrow night?"

Martin nodded: "We will be back by six tomorrow evening. Will it be possible for the meal to be brought here to my room?"

Minh laughed: "No problem at all. My Mom cooks not only for her boarders but also for people outside her boarding hostel. I will bring the meal to your room myself."

Nam commented: "This is no small victory. Thanks for your idea, Martin."

*

The long wait began without much hope and ended in disaster. Martin, Nam and Thu arrived at the medium's tent at eleven in the morning. They were served some food by noon time by her assistants. They sipped tea and waited, and waited and waited. Some people who came before them were taken to the medium's parlor. Then some of the people who came after them were invited in.

Thu was about to lose patience when four policemen came in. They went directly into the medium's parlor.

After they left, a trembling assistant of the medium came out to announce that the police had requested the medium to stop all activities. She apologized and asked everybody to leave.

So, "the tiny bit of hope" that Thu mentioned the day before when Martin just arrived in the lobby of the hotel was gone.

Thu's and Martin's quest had ended in an unmitigated defeat. Martin addressed silently to Mireille: "I have failed you. I have failed you."

Mireille's image that Martin saw clearly through the rain-splattered windshield of the cab was smiling. She said: "I am no longer here, Martin. I will always be with you and our children; and you never fail me as long as you still love me."

*

They sat in Martin's room around a small table. Thu exclaimed: "But this is a degustation menu. It's fantastic. You are genial, Martin!"

Nam said: "Martin, you must know that Thu and I came back to Vietnam with two goals in mind. We've failed to achieve any one of them. But thanks to you Thu is no longer devastated." He added teasingly: "She even smiles now." And Thu smiled. For the first time Martin saw her dimples and his heart missed a beat. Mireille's dimples!

He asked: "You mentioned two goals. I surmise that your first goal was to find the remains of your wife's parents. What was the second?"

Thu said: "I cannot have children. We have wanted for years to adopt a Vietnamese child. We thought that we had found a perfect child to adopt. We started sending money to the child and her family for the last two years. We found when we arrived in Saigon two weeks ago, that it was merely a scam. The pictures of the girl they sent us were fakes, and the family we corresponded with never had a daughter."

Nam noticed the sudden paleness of Martin's face. He asked: "Are you O.K. Martin?"

Martin nodded. He was silent for a moment, and then said simply: "Let's enjoy the dinner. After we finish eating, I will tell you about my adventure in Saigon."

*

Over the coffee Martin said: "I want to show you something." He walked to his suitcase, opened it, pulled out a manila envelope and walked back to the table. From the enveloped he took out two pictures and showed them to Nam and Thu. Thu exclaimed: "How beautiful she is! Is she one of your granddaughters?"

Martin felt a lump in his throat. He managed to say in the end: "Her name is Mai. She is a little girl looking for adoptive parents."

Thu touched Martin's hand and asked: "Are you facetious?"

Martin shook his head and looking Thu in her eyes, he said: "She asked me to adopt her. I told her I'm too old, too weak to raise another child. Her grandmother and she asked me help them find suitable adoptive parents for her. I told them that I knew few people and that I could not recommend anybody among the people I knew."

Thu grasped his hand and in an almost inaudible voice, she asked: "And now, you want to recommend us?"

Martin said: "She had a tragic childhood. Her father, a military surgeon was send to a re-education center after 1975. He was detained for twelve years then released when he was very sick. Her mother, a high-school teacher could not find a teaching position after 1975 and earned a living by working as part-time bookkeeper. Mai was born a couple of years after her father's release. She was two years old when her father died. She was nine when her mother died. Now she lives with her grandmother, who is a sidewalk *pho* vendor. But Mai was determined to be a physician like her father; and the only way for her to achieve that has been to be adopted by American adoptive parents."

Thu all in tears asked again: "Will you recommend us to her and her grandmother?"

Martin took another sip of coffee and nodded: "I feel like I have known you all my life. Yes, of course, I will recommend you."

Thu exclaimed: "Oh my God, this is miraculous! This is too much of a miracle!" Thu smiled through her tears. Again, that Mireille's smile!

She looked again at the pictures again and muttered: "Mai, my daughter, my beloved daughter! How beautiful you are!"

Nam said: "If she wants to become a physician, it will only depend on her. We have the means to send her to the best medical school."

Thu explained: "We worked hard for an IT company for five years after our graduation. Then we founded a company of our own. Three years ago we sold our company for a large amount of money and retired. Since then we have been living either at our principal home in Sedona or in an apartment we own in Phoenix."

Martin laughed: "You will do."

*

Two days later they took a flight to Saigon. Thu was radiant, and the more she smiled the more she looked like Mireille.

At Tan Son Nhat Airport Martin asked: "Why did you insist on staying at a cheap hotel like the Thuy Tien with me?"

Thu laughed: "Do you think that we will let you escape from us now that we are so close to our goal?"

Martin looked at her and laughed: "You will find out that you've gotten more than you bargained for by booking a room at the Thuy Tien Hotel."

Soon enough they were at the curb in front of the hotel. Martin stepped out of the car and looked. Mai saw him and yelled: "You are back!" She ran to him and put her arms around his waist, laughing and crying at the same time.

Thu trembled like a leaf. She asked: "Is this Mai? How come?" Martin laughed: "I omitted to tell you that the sidewalk *pho* stand I mentioned to you in Thanh Hoa is right in front of the hotel!"

Martin disengaged from Mai's embrace and said to her: "Take a hard look at this lady." Pointing at Nam who came to join them, he added: "And take a hard look at this gentleman. They are my friends, Nam and Thu. If you and your grandmother approve, they will be your adoptive parents."

Mai was petrified, so was her grandmother who had come closer. Thu knelt down and took Mai's hands in hers. She said: "I have seen your photos. Now I see you. Say yes, and will be happy forever."

Mai asked Martin, her lips trembling visibly: "Do you recommend them, Sir?"

Martin put his hand on her head and said: "Yes, Mai. I recommend them with all my heart."

Mai looked up to her grandmother, and when she received a nod from the old lady, said firmly: "Then, it's yes, Madam. Yes, I want to be your daughter." She looked up to Nam and repeated: "Yes, Sir, I want to be your daughter."

Thu said softly: "Mai, hold me. Hold me, my daughter."

Mai put her arms around Thu and smiled. For the first time Martin saw Mai's dimples.

*

Martin knew that somehow he had reached his goal. It did not matter anymore how many more days, months or years he would live. He had reached the goal of his life. He had been able to see almost ninety years of his life blended into a harmonious and comprehensible whole: past, present and future.

He called out softly: "Mireille, thank you." He distinctly heard her melodious and familiar voice: "You are welcome, Martin."

Wooden Flutes and Stone Clappers

Wooden flutes and stone clappers waken me at midnight
Moonlit hills like somnolent herds of cattle on my right
A path winding into the mist on my left, where am I?
Memories welling up , those we shared
before the time we said goodbye
My mind has wandered in endless quests
and followed shapeless dreams
Since you left! And questions without answer
came and are gone
Causing pain;   Stirrings of bats' wings in darkness!
So much pain, so many regrets
Since you left!
Sand dunes then sand dunes then again sand dunes.
You said, time has no hold on us. It is true.
But time destroys
what is left of our castles in the clouds.
Brick by brick, stone by stone
Dreams and realities alike came tumbling down
In a rain of dust. We should have known better.
The river follows the mist into the dark forest
Who am I to continue with this quest?
It would be easier if we call it quit and nurse
Our wounds, listening to the soothing sounds
Of flutes and clappers!

Monkey Watchtowers

Far faraway to the east, the dark blue Chimanimani Mountain Range stretched from north to south against a pale purple sky. The middleveld burned. The mopane trees and baobabs stood with weirdly twisted branches without leaves in the summer sun.

The small village in Masvingo Province close to the A1 Highway connecting Masvingo city and Beitbridge consisted of fewer than fifty miserable-looking thatch-roofed huts surrounded by maize fields.

A string of monkey watch towers, erected where the fields met the wild veld showed that beside the drought, the sudden invasions of voracious and voluminous velvet monkeys was the top worry of the villagers. Monkey watch towers were usually manned by very young boys or girls, who were conveniently out of school, on summer vacation as soon as the corn was about to be harvested. They would, at the first sight of the shoko or velvet monkey troops, beat the gongs and kettle drums at their disposal to alert the adults and scare away the monkeys.

Banga, the ten year old boy tried to keep his eyes open. The maize field extended from where the monkey tower stood up to the end of the mild slope. The slope stopped at a few yard from his home. The monkey watchtower looked down on the wilderness covered with thorny bushes from where the monkeys could approach the maze field without being detected. But those were in small bands easily scattered. The real danger was with larger troops of twenty or more. Those would gather and sit on the branches of nearby baobabs or mopane trees for a few minutes before they launched a general attack on a maize field. Banga like the other kids on the watchtowers were asked to watch closely the branches of the large trees. Failure to do so could lead to a devastating attack with maize fields completely destroyed in a few minutes, leading to hunger for the winter, and debts over many years.

"The maize field is our livelihood. It needs to be protected against the velvet monkeys. I will not let them come in without alerting my Mom", Banga kept repeating to himself. Soon enough, the warm breeze coming from the South and his own monotonous mantra overcame him and he dozed off. Banga, the Sword, mumbled in his sleep:" Where are you, Dad? Of course, he must be at that crappy beer bar again. Where are you, Dad? The monkeys are coming, how can I and Mom fight them back?"

Monkeys! He opened his eyes, fully awake now. On top of the hill his Mom was working at her vegetable patch. But the monkeys were already all over the maize field. He beat the gongs fiercely and shouted: *"Shoko! Shoko!"*

Now children on other watchtowers started beating their kettledrums and screamed:" Velvet monkeys!"

Banga saw his Mom coming down the slope with a big stick in her hand like a fury. There seemed to be two different packs of monkeys vying for Chidiwa's attention. While she was battling one pack, the other furiously attacked the maize cobs and the maize stalks. When she turned to the second pack, the first pack went back to destroying the maize field.

Then the big males got together and surrounded Chidiwa, showing threateningly their long and sharp teeth. Then one after another jumped at her. Their sheer weight –

some of them weighed over a hundred pounds – threw her at times on the ground. But her big stick continued to hit them even when she lay sprawling in the dust.

Banga climbed down the wooden ladder. He grabbed a stick and ran towards his Mom screaming:" It's my fault! It's my fault". With tears streaming down his face, he stood by his Mom and swung his stick fearlessly at the big monkeys.

Mother and son hit monkeys right and left. Fur flew, blood spilled, skulls broke, but the war was already lost. Looking past the large monkeys Chidiwa and Banga saw the last maize stalks trashed.

Chidiwa screamed:" I will kill you all". Her stick did kill one, then two monkeys. But snarling and "laughing", the monkeys were already retreating towards the spiky bushes at the end of the maize field. Then they disappeared with their loot.

A few neighbors arrived at the gate of the front yard and saw that it was too late. They watched Chidiwa and Banga a minute then decided to leave them alone. They knew how proud Chidiwa was and how she would hate to be seen by any one at that moment.

Chidiwa, unaware of the arrival and the withdrawal of her neighbors, threw her heavy stick away, sat down and with her hands over her face, she cried loudly. Banga sat down by her side and muttered: "It was my fault!" he kept repeating. After a while she turned to him and said: "No, it's not your fault!" She took his head and pressed it against her chest.

Looking up after another while, they saw Chatunga coming down the path. He walked fast in spite of his pronounced limp.

*

From where he was, at that crappy beer bar, Chatunga heard the alarm of gongs and kettle drums. Instinctively he knew that his maize field was under attack.

He got up and paid the one-eyed bar owner then got out. He looked down at his left leg with disgust. In the last days of the war, battalion commander Chatunga was hit by a bullet that broke his femur. The fracture was treated by a clumsy nurse as no surgeon was around. He came back to the village after the war and was received like a hero, a hero who walked with a limp.

It was his limp that prompted Chief Zuma to ask for an astronomical *roora* when the wounded warrior wanted to get married to Chidiwa. Indeed, he asked for five heads of cattle. How could Chatunga pay for five heads of cattle? How could a penniless veteran pay for them?

The local leaders of the ruling party, ZANU-PF (Zimbabwe African National Union- Patriotic Front) came to the rescue. They talked to Chief Zuma about Chatunga's past services to the nation and told him that even with a limp Chatunga could at any time obtained a top appointment in the government.

Chief Zuma was astute enough, however, to see that local members of the ZANU delegation were not so fond of Chatunga. Some even could barely hide their antipathy towards him and their fear that he would become a ZANU leader again and would sweep them away without any difficulty.

Chief Zuma promised to reconsider Chatunga's suit, but did nothing of the kind. He even looked actively for a younger man for his daughter.

Hurt in his pride, Chatunga was about to renounce to pursue the matter. But Chidiwa stepped into the fight and told her father that she would run away with Chatunga if the Chief continued to create problem for her marriage with the former battalion commander.

Now walking home from the beer bar, Chatunga remembered that and felt weak inside. He had forgotten all about her battle to get married to him. He had neglected his family by allowing self-pity to take over his mind and his heart. He had sunk low. He had been drinking more and more heavily, and spending more and more time at the beer bar.

He now remembered the pride on her face on their wedding day. It was as if she had attained the goal of her life. Yet, she was a little girl when he departed from the village and joined the revolutionary army. She waited for him for over five years. Why didn't she see that he went home a handicapped?

He had never asked her why.

He had never asked her why she had harassed chief Zuma until her father consented to give her the piece of land that had in good years and in bad provided her family with its livelihood (She did not show any regret when she had to clear and cultivate that land by herself).

Then Banga came.

He remembered how proudly she had asked him to name their son *Banga*, the Sword. "It's appropriate for the son to be named The Sword, when his father is *Chatunga*, the Warrior", she said.

He remembered that he had called her everyday Chidiwa and forgotten that it meant *graceful*.

100

How could he let her work by herself year in year out on their plot of land while he was at the bar, drinking beer with the money she had worked so hard for, the money that she gave him without grudge? He wanted to know now.

*

What had happened to his maize field? Maybe, his wife and his son had been successful in beating back the monkeys. And then maybe they had been defeated and the maize field was gone now. He started running ignoring the pain in his fractured femur.

*

At a glance he saw the extent of the damages.

He saw his wife with disheveled hair, the picture of despair.

He saw his son standing by her side looking at him like he would look at a stranger.

He walked slowly toward them feeling their pain. He realized that he had not looked straight into Chidiwa's eyes for months, maybe years. She suddenly ran to him and hit him repeatedly on the chest, screaming: "Where were you? Where were you, when we needed you?"

He held her tight and in a minute she went limp in his arms. She said weakly: "We will go hungry this winter." He said: "No, we won't."

She said:" Then I would have to my father and beg him on my knees ..." He said firmly: "No, you won't have to do that." It gave him pain that she accepted to humiliate herself before her father, at the same time it gave him joy to see that she would do it without hesitation for Banga and for him.

Now she looked into his eyes. She was searching for that young man she had fallen in love with when she was barely fifteen, that young revolutionary, that young commander. What she saw was more than that. She saw tenderness, she saw remorse. Then she saw, oh my God, she saw love.

She started sobbing and his hands went up and smoothed her hair, and touched her face. She asked with fear and irrepressible joy: "Are you going into politics? The elections will take place next month." With all her heart, she wished that he would say no. She had seen enough of the corruption and arrogance of the new people in power.

He put his hand over her mouth and said: "I know that if I want to get into politics *they* would gladly put me in a position of power. But no! I have only disgust for the people in power nowadays. I was a hero. I was *their* hero. I led the fight when they all went to Zambia or England to be safe. I did not mind their choice of being in a safe place to give orders to commanders who stayed behind and fought, like me. But I could not stand what *they* did since our Party took power: *They* pushed the Ndebele people into rebellion, *they* slaughtered over 20, 000 Ndebele soldiers and civilians. *They* tortured tens of thousands more in detention camps. *They* did that when the entire people of Zimbabwe should be celebrating our independence and liberation as a united nation."

She had been waiting for *this* to come out: she had been waiting for him to tell her his innermost thoughts and shed light on his behavior since he came back from the war. "The devastation of our maize field can wait, she said to herself, what he is saying is far more important.'

She asked "You are embittered by the *Gukurahundi?*" She felt revulsion race through his body: "Yes *they* had the nerve to call the massacre of the Ndebele people, their comrades-in-arms "the early rain which washes away the chaff before the spring rains"; for me, the massacre ended my sympathy for "the revolution". I don't want to have anything to do with *them,* ever again."

"Was that why you started drinking?" she asked timorously. He hesitated a while then said: "Yes and no, the drinking started when I saw the emptiness of the days ahead of me when revolution had been betrayed. I did not see how I could have a life without the guiding light of true revolution."

She asked him: "How about us? Banga and I, aren't we enough for you to rebuild your life on?" He was silent for a long moment. Tremulously she searched her mind and wondered whether she had hurt his feelings with her awkward words.

He said: "Since I was a little boy, revolution, liberation and freedom were my drivers. I was passionate when I fought for those abstract ideals. I have for so long doubted that I could feel as much passion for you and Banga. That is, until today!"

She hung on to him while pulling her son to her. The three of them stood motionless under the sun. Only a few yards away, the devastated maize field no longer had any meaning at all. Chidiwa no longer felt anger, terror, despair or worry. She felt only contentment and yes, happiness. She was happier than ever before. The moment had all the quality of eternity.

She asked, breaking the spell: "How do we face winter?"

He lifted her chin up and laughed: "Do you know how my people called me during the war?" She shook her head. He said:" They called me "The commander who feeds the whole army".

Of course, she had heard all about it. She asked with lights of amusement dancing in her eyes: "Really?"

Chatunga tousled Banga's hair and said: "I was the best hunter and the best fisherman in the whole army. I knew where to dig for edible roots, where to find edible leaves, and how to turn poisonous fruit into edible fruit. I was the one who knew which mushrooms to eat and which ones to avoid touching."

More lights of amusement danced in Chidiwa's eyes. She asked: "So where should we begin and what should we expect?"

Chatunga laughed: "We shall begin by building a smokehouse. There are plenty of games around here, so expect to see lots of venison and wild hog meat. Expect lots of smoked fish, salted fish and brined fish. Expect a lot of pickled shellfish..."

Chidiwa laughed: "Stop right there. Don't you see poor Banga salivating and drooling? Are you sure you will stop drinking? Will you have the courage to go hunting and fishing every day?"

Chatunga did not reply. But Chidiwa, looking into his eyes saw there more than a promise. She lowered her head and stood motionless, allowing him to peer at her as long as he wanted. There was a glow in her face that he hadn't seen for years.

He said:" I am sorry Chidiwa!"

She smiled and shook her head: "For what *mudikanwi* (my love)?"

The little Banga chimed in: "Sorry for what *Warrior*? Sorry for what, *Commander who feeds the whole army*?"

Chatunga gathered the little boy in his arms while he continued to watch his wife. Finally she said:" Stop looking at me like that or I will burst into tears."

He remembered now that indeed he had never seen her cry.

*

Chidiwa knew that to stop drinking cold turkey would have consequences. For several days and nights she watched her husband go through the bad mood, sweating and fever, but he never went into shock. Apparently he did not drink too much at the beer bar.

She was astute enough to get Banga out of the way whenever his father had a bad moment. She felt more and more admiration for her *Warrior* who struggled on without complaining.

*

Though Chidiwa had not entertained the best rapports with her father, hunting on Chief Zuma's private and tribal lands was open to her and her husband. Chatunga was free to roam those immense stretches of land. No bureaucrat at the local Wildlife Management Authority found it wise to give any trouble to Chatunga when he applied for permits and licenses for rifle hunting and bow hunting, and fishing for himself and for his wife.

105

Building a brand new and large smokehouse was fun. Chidiwa and Banga took care of the walls while Chatunga put up the roof. Chidiwa kept saying: "Why so big a smokehouse?" Chatunga simply laughed her off: "You still don't believe I can fill up this smokehouse with food, do you?"

But he knew he had to prove to her that the reputation he had built for himself in the army was well deserved.

So, every day before sunrise, Chatunga and Chidiwa (and Banga during the weekends and his frequent vacations) would leave their hut and headed for their hunting grounds or for one of the small rivers that feed Lake Mitirikwe teeming with fish.

Chidiwa was always beautiful in her hunting garb and Chatunga stopped walking from time to time to admire the way she carried the compound bow on her back and the side quiver with a half dozen arrows.

Banga preferred to wear a waterfowl life vest.

The three of them enjoyed the walk as much as the actual hunting or fishing.

After sunrise, they would sit down by the side of a footpath and ate their copious breakfast. Then another long walk, before they reached destination.

Both Chidiwa and Banga would let Chatunga do most of the shooting and fishing. They helped him with the bagging and carrying home the game or the catch of the day.

When they went big-game hunting, they would stop by Chief Zuma's home and borrow a jeep as a warthog or antelope could not be carried on their shoulders over long distances.

106

In the winter they stopped all those hunting and fishing trips. But they had plenty of things to do at home.

Banga found more time to take care of the few heads of cattle grazing on their former maize field. Chidiwa thought that with time they would have a sizable herd of cattle.

In their hunting trips Chatunga recognized some large stones for what they were: Zimbabwean jade. He went to Harrare and came back with a jade carver. He built a house for the carver and asked him to teach villagers how to carve warthogs, elephants, hippos and monkeys. Little by little the village changed its look. No more maize fields. No more monkey watchtowers. No longer a precarious life based on one single precarious crop.

Chief Zuma found somewhere in his heart a tiny bit of generosity. He lent money to those villagers who wanted to buy cattle. He spent his own money to build a store for villagers who wanted to sell their jade carvings to tourists.

*

Chidiwa soon realized that Chatunga had stopped having problems with alcohol withdrawal and that he was a changed man. That should have made her most happy, yet she was a little scared, as alcohol had for so long assuaged his pain and his frustration. Could he stay sober and happy at the same time?

She approached him one day and asked him timorously: "Are you sure that this kind of life is satisfying for you? Do Banga and I make you forget about the outside world?"

Chatunga laughed and said: "Woman, don't you know that the outside world is in fact very small and that the world you and Banga represent is immense for me?"

Chidiwa said: "You are the Warrior, Chatunga. How can you be comfortable with your new fetters?"

Chatunga burst laughing again: "So, you are my new fetters? I thought that you were the rest of the warrior."

His words threw her into total confusion, especially when Banga piped in: "What does father mean by "the rest of the warrior", Mom?"

She said, blushing: "It's a bad word, a very bad word, Banga; don't you ever dare use it."

There Comes a Time

In memory of Tom Barnes,
USMC, USAID, USDS, UNHCR, ICMC, my friend

There comes a time when pain wouldn't go away,

When tired eyes barely see the light of day,

When colors fade and a jungle drum beats like the heavy

Hammer striking at the brain and the heart,

And when the faces of loved ones became hazy,

Then, it is time to go, my dear

To where the voice of pine trees is fresh and clear,

Back to that beach with white rocks and emerald water,

Back to the time where regrets were sweet and dreams
mattered.

For a long time, we, your friends, will not forget

The nightly screams of seagulls over Leman Lake;

For a long time we will, for old time's sake,

Stroll the beaches where night and day reach out until they
meet

One minute, in glorious twilight

Then yield the place to total darkness.

For the longest time, we will visit the sites of your pilgrimages

Where multitudes were slaughtered while we stood helpless

And watched the corruption of the monsters on stages

Swallowing entire nations. For the longest time we will witness

Like you did, the long march of survivors winding in the wilderness

Finding no asylum or mercy anywhere.

Yet, there were places that had given you strength,

There were moments that had made you shake with happiness.

We will go back there too and visit at length

and treasure the short moments where we and you had found blessedness.

You the yellow- haired boy laughing in the field of golden wheat,

You the young man crouched in the trench strewn with body parts,

You the quiet observer of man's ambitions, envy and greed

You, the helpless helper with a broken heart

Rest, dear friend, until again we will all meet

To chat and laugh, and remember under distant stars.

The Drunken Priest

He knew right away that the Bishop of the Diocese of Mahenge as well as the Cardinal Archbishop of the Ecclesiastical Province of Dar-es-Salaam had sent him to the poorest, the tiniest and the remotest parish in all Tanzania. But he didn't care. It was better to be in a parish than in a cloistered monastery. And there was reason enough for them to force him into the strictest monastic life. He was the shameless drunken Priest who once ran naked in the streets of Mahenge.

His bishop believed that he was a hopeless case and expected him to decline rapidly as he drowned himself deeper and deeper in cheap wine.

Father Elias Sanga staggered into the sacristy. Ben, his altar boy, was already vested in his black cassock and yellowed surplice full of holes. Ben was always barefooted but the priest never seemed to notice such an impropriety. Actually, he never dared raise a question, fearing that the boy would cry and say he had no money to buy sandals.

The priest himself wore a pair of creaky sandals: they squished at every step he made and would have been a distraction in the church if it were not for the fact that very few people came to attend *his* Mass at Our Lady of Assumption Church.

*

The three Little Sisters of the Poor, who were supposed to serve Fr. Elias Sanga, had traveled to Mahenge and given an unforgiving situation report to the Bishop. They were authorized to attend mass at Ubungo parish three miles away from the church of our Lady of Assumption. They were also authorized to abstain from washing Father Sanga's clothes.

They continued to cook for him though, but they never partook a meal with him. Three times a day they brought a tray of food to the rectory. The food they cooked for him was somewhat superior to their own fare, and Fr. Elias Sanga never complained about its lack of variety.

The finances of the parish were quite simple. Half of the money collected on Sundays would go to the priest and the sisters' food; half would go into church maintenance, which meant candles, and mass wine.

The priest's quite modest salary was also divided into two parts: one part was used primarily for the purchase of a few bottles of cheap wine and the other part for miscellaneous expenses such as the Sisters' trip to Mahenge.

Fortunately, the Sisters received from time to time a supplement of food and money from their Mother House. Without those supplements it would be difficult to see how the priest and nuns make ends meet.

*

After mass the priest used to ask Ben to follow him to the rectory. He liked to give the boy some biscuits. They boy used to eat them slowly nad Fr. Elias had all the time in the world to eat his breakfast in the presence of the boy and chat with him about what was going on in the parish. The priest believed that the reason kept the child while he ate his

112

breakfast was his wish to know more about the daily life of his parishioners.

But the true reason he wanted the boy to be there was that without another presence at the rectory he might end his breakfast with a few glasses of wine.

That morning the boy did not tarry with him. He said his mother needed him at home, and Fr. Elias ended his breakfast quickly. As soon as the boy got out of the rectory with his biscuits, Fr. Elias poured himself two large glasses of wine. The wine absorbed so early in the morning got him a little dizzy.

He decided to take a walk. From the rectory, Fr Elias took a footpath across the little vegetable patch tended by the Sisters, then up a little slope, a kind of bushy no man's land and ended up in the district road.

It was not much of a road. It was a deserted dirt road with plenty of large and treacherous holes in the middle of it. The daily bus going to Ubungo was sometimes trapped in those holes, and each time all the travelers in the bus needed to come down and push it along with the bus comptroller while the driver swore and changed screeching gears, swore and prayed the Christian God, the Muslim Allah and the indigenous *Mungu to* get his bus out of the hole.

*

It was very early and the night fog was not entirely lifted. "Very low visibility", Fr. Elias said to himself. He walked cautiously, praying the rosary absent-mindedly. He was vaguely aware that he was inebriate, but he continued with his prayers "*gratia plena, Dominus tecum,* so what? I have always been a drunk, *benedicta tu in mulieribus,* I am the Drunken Priest, remember?" His foot hit something on the road. He staggered and fell down. At first, he thought it was a dead dog. Then he realized it was a dead boy, an albino boy.

Then he had a panic attack.

He knelt down next to the body. He knew that the boy did not die a natural death. In most countries in Africa the albinos were considered animals of bad omen. They were constantly driven out of urban centers, often beaten up by children as well as adults and sometimes killed pitilessly.

Bathed with sweat Fr. Elias half raised the body of the albino boy and holding him tight, he started singing softly. Where had he learned to sing *bongo flava* tunes like that? He sat there in the mud singing softly with closed eyes to the boy.

He was not aware of a crowd of people gathered around him. They watched him intently but did not make any noise. They just stood there and watched the scene.

A rainstorm came and went. Soaking wet, Fr. Elias remained there and kept singing to the boy. The crowd also drenched by the rainstorm stood, entranced, until the constable from Ubungo came.

Fr. Elias tried to fight the constable when the latter wanted to pull the albino from him. But he was too weak to fight for long. He let go the boy and tried to get up. He found that all the joints of his body were ankylosed from head to toe. He couldn't get up. When the bystanders tried to help him get back on his feet, he said softly: "Let me be. I want to go on praying for the little lad some more." But he could not stay on his knees. He sat in the mud and lowered his head.

But he could not pray. He started feeling an agonizing pain spread from his stomach to his chest. He became feverish, and his hands trembled. He sweated profusely and kept mumbling to himself: "I am no good."

It was strange that the villagers and his parishioners did not leave him there to himself. They had done so every time he fell and could not get up when drunk. "Why do they stay and look at me with those eyes?"

It was then that the Sisters came back after attending Mass in Ubungo. They saw the crowd standing around Fr. Elias. They were both angry and ashamed. Sister Teresa asked scornfully:" He fell again, didn't he?" To her surprise, many in the crowd put a finger on their lips advising her to shut her mouth. Someone explained for the benefit of the Sisters: "He found a dead albino boy right here. He would not let go of the body until the constable arrived. Then he stayed there to pray."

Sister Lois exclaimed: "He is going into shock, my God. Can somebody help?"

Two strong parishioners pulled Fr. Elias up and half-carried, half-dragged the poor priest to the rectory.

For the three Sisters it was amazing that the crowd did not jeer at him, nor laugh at him. It was amazing!

Other parishioners carried Fr. Elias to his bed and looked at the convulsing priest with fear. Sister Anne-Mary said: "Maybe we should give him some wine."

Sister Teresa reluctantly poured a half glass of wine and raising the priest head, she pressed the rim of the glass to his mouth. Fr. Elias raised his hand apparently to steady the glass.

He saw the red blood on his hand, the blood of the albino boy, and the red wine. He shook his head and retched violently. He managed to say in the end: "No wine, please."

Summoning all his strength he said:" Now, everybody, please leave. I will be all right. But I need to be alone."

The Sisters found three blankets and threw them on him.

Then they and everybody else left.

*

He knew that he needed to stay in bed. But he had to do something first. He managed to get his feet down to the ground and attempted to stand up. He was so weak that he was afraid that his legs or his knees would snap and break into pieces. Somehow, that did not happen.

He let his body go so that he fell on the side of the table. The bottle of wine was still there. Sister Teresa had not taken it away.

For the longest time Fr.Elias clung to the side of the table and watched the content of the bottle. He did not see wine. He saw darkened blood. The blood of the albino boy. He remembered how in one of his quite recent homilies, delivered without much thought, he did mention the supertitious fear and hatred of the albinos. He had said: " Such superstition must have no place in the heart of Christians."

Through the fog of alcohol he seemed to see that all of a sudden his parishioners became attentive. But right there he had lost the thread of his thinking and he had to talk about something else.

Now he regretted he dis not have the courage and the lucidity to talk more about the subject: He had seen albinos being chased away with brooms, sticks and stones. He had seen albino boys beaten unconscious.

116

And now, they had killed the albino boy.

He saw himself an accomplice of the crime.

He mumbled: " God, please forgive me." There was an image of the Blessed Heart of Jesus on the wall facing him. Fr. Elias shook his head: " No, God, I should not think only of myself. Forgive all of us, oh God, because we are all of us accomplices of the crime."

*

The packed church with the three Sisters in the front pew waited for Fr. Elias to start his homily. The priest was unsteady on his feet but his hands did not tremble too much.

Fr. Elias cleared his throat and started speaking. At first he did not have the courage to look at the faces in front of him. He looked into the void, and his voice was high-pitched. Then, little by little he somehow found the anger and the pain in him and shouted: "Look at me! Look at your miserable pastor! Brothers and Sisters, look at the drunk in front of you!"

There were uneasy stirrings in the congregation, but the priest went on: "Follow my example, drink yourselves to death; drink yourselves to damnation. Walk always with a bottle in your hand, or better pressed to your chest; spend your time, brothers, at the bars, and let your women work like slaves on your little patches of land, and eke out a living for you and your families! Yes, they are your slaves; they are born to work for you and the children. Enjoy yourselves!"

He stopped, out of breath, for a while, and then shouted again: "Follow my example! Keep your mouth shut when people are beating up innocent albino children. Keep your mouth shut when barbarians among you kill them supposedly because they would bring you bad luck! Follow my example!"

Lowering his voice he said: " Yesterday the Bishop came. Yes, he came all the way from the City of Mahenge. He asked me to go to a Rehab Center in Dar-es-Salaam to purify myself, to get rid once for all by drinking habit. But I said to him...Do you know what I said to him? I said: " Your Excellency, I am too far gone for any treatment. But I know that the dead albino boy, the murdered albino boy will prevent me from ever drinking alcohol again."

" He said:" Don't be stubborn. You will go through very bad days if you stop drinking. You need medical help. You need nurses and doctors to help you when you have withdrawal symptoms, when your body starts trembling uncontrollably..."

"I thanked him again, but I am not going. Your know why? Because I have a bunch of bastards like me whom I have to deal with in the years or months that remain for me to live. I said to him: " Excellency, you have sent me to the right place; I want to live here for the rest of my short life."

"And the Bishop is gone. So, here we are, you and I Bothers and Sisters, all accomplices of a murder, and maybe other murders that we have forgotten. You are here with me Brothers, you unrepentant alcoholics. May God forgive us and give us opportunities to redeem ourselves. I am afraid though that God will not come close to us because of our stench."

"If I were you I would give the albino boy a decent burial when the police was done with him. I suggest that his grave will be visited every day. Brothers and Sisters, bring flowers to the grave whenever you can"

He stopped and collapsed.

The Sisters and his parishioners ran to him. With a surhuman effort, Fr. Elias opened his eyes and said to Sister

Lois: " Bring me the offerings, the bread, wine and water." Sister Lois complied and Fr. Elias consecrated the bread and the wine. He said:" This is Sunday, they have to attend the whole Mass." With tears in her eyes Sister Lois nodded understanding.

The priest then lay inert and they carried him to his rectory.

Once he was tucked comfortably in his bed the Sisters led the congregation back to the church and led it in the recitation of the rosary. Then Sister Lois went up to the altar and took the consecrated bread and wine to the rail seperating the sanctuary from the congregation.

Aided by Ben, the altar boy, she gave communion to the parishioners. There was hearty singing at the end of the Mass.

*

Sister Lois said: "The whole parish is a rehab center now. The Bishop has dispatched a Catholic doctor and our Mother House has sent in five Sisters who are certified nurses. Every man in the parish wants to quit drinking cold turkey. We use part of our house here as a clinic. "

Sister Anne-Mary said: "The Bishop told us that what you did was like a miracle."

Fr. Elias said gruffly: "Soon enough I will be walking around with a halo over my head."

He laughed but the Sisters did not laugh. They introduced ceremoniously the doctor and the five new Sisters.

Fr. Elias said: "I know I passed out. But how many days did I sleep?"

Dr. Davis Gurnah said: "You slept for five days. I have no recollection of any case like yours. You were fed intravenously. You had some bad dreams, not real nightmares. Strangely enough you stopped sweating after the second day."

Fr. Elias asked: "May I get up now."

Dr. Gurnah nodded: "You may be very hungry but you can walk out into the garden. Fresh air may help."

Sister Teresa handed him his cassock that had been well washed and well ironed. He put it on and headed toward the door. At the threshold he turned around and remarked:" The world is still here, thank God!"

*

It didn't take a genius to figure out who the murderer was. It was Joseph Mdee, a boy of eleven, whose house was not far from the rectory.

As soon as he knew that the police had come and taken Joseph away to a juvenile detention center in Mahenge, Fr. Elias asked Dr. Gurnah to drive him there.

Dr. Gurnah stunned by what he had seen since his arrival with the five Sisters-nurses to the Parish of Our Lady of Assumption wanted to know: "What are you going to tell the boy?"

Fr. Elias laughed: "If this happened a month ago, I would tell him lots of things; then I would give him a rosary and ask him to pray for his soul. But now... maybe I don't have to tell him anything. He may have a need to talk to me. Maybe I will simply listen to what he has to say."

*

Joseph sat on the floor. He did not get up when the pastor and the doctor were ushered in. Though there were a few chairs scattered around the room, Fr. Elias sat down on the floor next to the boy while Dr. Gurnah stood by awkwardly and watched the boy and the priest.

Neither the priest nor the boy seemed ready to talk. They sat with their head hung low. Dr Gurnah was afraid that nothing was going to break that silence.

Then all of a sudden, the boy whispered: "I was drunk!" The priest did not seem to hear. He leaned over and put his ear closer to the boy. Joseph repeated: "I said I was drunk!"

"How come you were drunk?"

"My dad came home drunk, with the bottle half full. He passed out, while holding the bottle. I was afraid that he would drop the bottle. So I took the bottle out of his hand. I had tried to drink before. Each time I had gotten sick. I hated alcohol. But that night I looked at my dad and said: "So you son of a bitch, you get drunk again hah! You get drunk, then beat me up hah! But not tonight! Tonight you cannot beat me up because you are so drunk that you pass out. So let me get drunk. When I am drunk I will pick up a big stick and beat you up!"

"You got drunk for real?"

"Yes, I got drunk for good. I drank one sip, then another, then another. I took a broom with a long handle and hit my dad with it. Once, twice, I don't know. Maybe I did not hit hard enough because he did not stir or anything. I said to myself:" I got to go to the yard and get a big stick. I remembered I had seen a big broken branch on top of the hedge. Maybe a couple of days ago there had been a big wind. The wind had broken the branch from the big tree on the side of the road."

"How did you find your way to the hedge? It was very dark that night."

"No, it was not dark. The front door of our home was wide open, and there was a kerosene lamp on the table. So I saw everything clearly from the house, to the hedge, then to the road. I grabbed the branch and was about to run to the house with it to beat up my Dad... But then, I saw walking on the road that albino boy."

The boy stopped and started sobbing. The priest did not ask any question, he just sat there looking into the void.

After a long while the boy asked: " I will go straight to hell, huh?"

The priest did not answer him and the boy started sobbing again.

Dr. Gurnah intervened: " Father, tell him that he will not go straight to hell if he repents, please."

The priest looked up and Dr. Gurnah saw in his eyes such pain that he was bewildered.

Finally, the priest said: " You are only eleven; so there will be no juvenile jury trial. A judge will sentence you to several years of probation and to several years of public service. The parish council and I will petition the judge to let you serve your years of public service at the church. You will work at the church half-time. You will promise us that you will not run away and that you will work hard to redeem yourself. By the way, one of ths chores you will have is to take care of the albino boy's grave."

The boy threw his arms around the priest's neck and cried.

When he finished crying, the boy asked again: "Will I go straight to hell, Father?"

The priest shook his head thoughtfully and said: "Heaven and Hell can wait, you know, let us live our life as decently as we could first."

*

The Bishop was intimidated. He saw improvements everywhere in the little parish. He looked at the priest who walked beside him. He said: "The Cardinal Archbishop of Dar-es-Salaam wants you to be one of his Auxiliary Bishops. He only waits for your acceptance to petition Rome for that. He asked me to announce to you the good news."

The priest did not show any sign of surprise. He kept walking in silence. Finally he turned to the Bishop: "His Eminence of the Cardinal is fortunate. He never was an alcoholic, and probably has not had any close friend or relative who is at one time or another alcoholic. That is why he wants me to be a Bishop. Do you know, Excellency, that an alcoholic is an alcoholic for life? I drunken priest is a big scandal. But how about a drunken bishop? The scandal would be enormous. Do you really believe that I will be sober for good and that there will not be relapses?"

The Bishop smiled: "You are not a common man who quits drinking all of a sudden. You are Fr. Elias who has rehabilitated every drunk in his parish."

Fr. Elias shook his head: "They are not rehabilitated, Bishop. They are all vulnerable. They are vulnerable for life. Like me. They need me here. And I need them. Do you know when I have the greatest difficulty in fighting to stay sober? In the morning, right after Mass, right after I touch the consecrated wine, even so lightly, with my lips. I have asked my parishioners to pray for me every morning for that reason. Yes, I need them, and they need me. Together we will fight against our addiction, maybe successfully for a day at a time. Please tell His Eminence the Cardinal that I am most grateful for his consideration, but that my place is here. Bishop, please, don't take me away from here. "

The Bishop nodded and they walked on. He knew that he would have no problem explaining to the Cardinal why Fr. Elias turned down the offer to be a bishop. He smiled to himself: "It is difficult, he thought, "to fight against a living saint".

The Bishop was wrong when he thought he was talking to a living saint. Fr. Elias had several relapses. But he got up and stayed sober for a longer time after each relapse.

He and his parishioners are not living saints; all of them remain dangerously vulnerable, humble, and shamelessly tenacious. Together they are building one of the most vibrant communities in their region. But there was no living saint among them.

Tears of a Hutu Priest

The moon was dim. Black clouds sailed through the darkened sky. In the distance the angry red glow of a large fire continued to spread uncontrolled. The tired tomtom still resounded in the jungle, yet it was no longer a call for help. Its slow beats resounded more and more like one wave after another of deprecations and strangled curses.

The priest stood in the shadow, half hidden behind a large pillar. I sat on the low wall of the balcony facing him obliquely and listening to his deep voice. The monotone of the evening prayers said by sleepy seminarians in the nearby chapel did not cover his words but rather added a new tonality to them

I first met Evergiste in Rome at the Pontifical Lateran University a year earlier. He was then preoccupied with the final draft of his doctoral dissertation. Later I met him when he had been called back from Rome by his bishop in Kabgayi. He was our house guest in Geneva, Switzerland, for a week, together with a Tutsi colleague. Our conversations steered clear away from the apocalyptic genocides that had occurred recently in Rwanda and in Burundi.

He left Rome without much regret. Anyway, he had completed his dissertation on "Saint Augustine and Africa" and defended it successfully. But according to his own candid evaluation of the dissertation, it was a more convincing homage to Africa and a less convincing assertion of the *enormous* influence that Africa had on Saint Augustine.

125

For years I had tried to avoid meeting a Hutu unaccompanied by a Tutsi and vice-versa. The presence of both sides usually tempered the vehemence of their words. Meeting with only one side might drive you to insanity. The atrocities committed: the slaughter of over 20,000 Hutu in Burundi in 1972, then the holocaust of over half a million Tutsis and *moderate* Hutu in 1994 and then, the revenge killings of Hutu following the holocaust had left deep scars in the conscience of the world.

On that night in Lusaka, I broke that promise to myself: I was facing a Hutu without a Tutsi counterpart. For half an hour, Evergiste was quite entertaining: I was intrigued by his meandering thoughts and found charm and acute intelligence in his self-deprecating remarks. For half an hour we did not talk about Hutu and Tutsi. We were not in Hutu lands anyway, as we were neither in Rwanda nor in Burundi, nor in Uganda or Tanzania. We had come here in Lusaka, Zambia for an international conference on refugees and migrants in Africa. Fresh out from Rome, Evergiste had been asked by his bishop to represent Rwanda for all Rwandans at the meet before heading home.

But then his mind shifted. Every word Evergiste said sank into me like a slash of machete among the clamors of hundreds of thousand lives lost in Hutu lands and strangely enough mixed with the outcry of the millions of Cambodians slaughtered by the Khmer Rouge twenty years earlier. Yet somehow I knew I had to listen to him because he was a man in great pain.

I asked him: "Do you hate the Tutsi?"

He was silent for a long time. Then, instead of answering my question, he said: "Kabgayi is a beautiful city viewed from any direction. If you stand on the hills in the south and look at the Basilica of Our Lady then at the faraway

126

mountains your heart will be filled with peace and contentment. If you stand on the mountains looking down at the huddled city you will feel the same way."

I waited patiently until he said: "The Tutsi killed three Hutu bishops and ten Hutu priests two months ago a few miles South of Kabgayi."

I had read newspapers and learned about the tragedy. But it was a fact that Hutu paramilitaries had killed over 60,000 Tutsi just before that.

I did not expect to hear him say: "One day, I do not know when, you may see me in the streets of Kabgayi with a blood stained machete in my hand."

I was so horrified by his words that I could not say anything for a while. He seemed to wait for my response, but receiving none, he breathed hard and added as a lame excuse: "I grew up in Kabgayi, went to the seminary there, was ordained priest there at the Basilica of Our Lady. My bishop indicated in his letter to me in Rome that I would be the Father Superior of the Seminary of Kabgayi...and I guess I will die soon in Kabgayi... with a blood-stained machete in my hand."

I cried out: "How could you say such a thing! You are a priest. You are a theologian. You will be Father Superior of the Kabgayi Seminary! Don't you see how much hope your Bishops have been placing on you?"

He said: "It's easy for you to condemn me. What do you know about human cruelty and human madness? How could you understand the hellish cycle of murder and revenge and bloody battles in a civil war? "

He looked at me intently again and suddenly remembered where I came from. Realizing his awful *faux pas*, he said: "I am sorry. You must have known all of that in Vietnam."

No. I could never know. Each war is different.

*

I said: "I came from a country where countless people were slaughtered by one side or another for over 30 years of war. I have more than once experienced some of your pain and your anger. Yet I cannot in anyway know what you feel, what a common Hutu or common Tutsi feels. Granted, for many centuries Hutu lived under Tutsi domination. Granted Tutsi kings and Tutsi lords impaled Hutu sometimes without provocation. It is however a fact that in this century the Hutu killed over a million Tutsi within a few months in 1994. Over a million Evergiste! Over sixty percent of all the Tutsi then residing in Rwanda!

Evergiste stepped back further into the shadow. In a strangled voice he said: " Should we go to the chapel and pray now before we go to bed?"

Indeed the singsong of the evening prayers had stopped. We would have all the chapel to ourselves. He reluctantly followed me into the small chapel. He doggedly stayed in the dark rows of pews in the rear. I left him there and advanced far to the front pews.

In Lusaka a rainstorm could start in a few minutes. Soon enough lightning and thunder were underway. Soon enough large raindrops splashed on banana leaves on both sides of the chapel.

Even in the loud cacophony of the rainstorm I could hear Evergiste's sighs, then his silence, then his uncontrollable sobbing.

*

The refectory was clean but the food was lousy. Three times a day we were served exactly the same stuff over and over again. It was potato soup with a tiny hint of shredded chicken. We sat on long benches and pretended we were interested in food.

I saw Evergiste come in, stay a few minutes then get out. I know he would be ambushing me outside and so tarried as long as I could. But then in a moment the morning session of the conference would start. I sighed and got out.

I was right. He was there waiting for me in the hall. His eyes were red. He looked at me for the longest time then he said with tears running down his prematurely wrinkled cheeks: "Kabgayi two years ago was given the chance to become a refugee center, a safe zone. Yes, a safe zone for Tutsi refugees. But *we*, the Hutu of Kabgayi turned that safe zone into a death camp. Every morning *we* marched bunches of young Tutsi out into the field and slaughtered them with machetes. *We* even buried many of them alive. At night, our paramilitaries went from tent to tent and raped the Tutsi girls and women. *We* were bloodthirsty savages and then when Tutsi militiamen defeated *our* forces and slaughtered us, *we* called them savages."

How could he reverse his thinking like that in one night? No, he had had those thoughts before I talked to him the night before. Those thoughts had been killing him and he had thrashed about against the Tutsi.

But now he was in reverse mode and I did not think that his new attitude was healthy either.

He pronounced *nous* (we) and *notre* (our) with such intensity that I wanted to scream: "You cannot assume all the sins of the Hutus. Only Christ can."

129

I put my hand on his arm to calm him down. But he wasn't to be controlled. He made a series of gurgling sounds and the only thing I could understand was: "How could I help redeem Kabgayi? Could it be redeemed?"

*

Evergiste was killed a few months later somewhere south of Kabgayi. But not with a machete in his hand! He was killed by a group of Hutu who were disgusted with him because he had dared to talk about a possible reconciliation between Tutsi and Hutu. He should have left Kabgayi when they started labeling him as a *moderate Hutu.*

Without knowing it he had assumed all the sins of the Hutu nation-- and those of the Tutsi too.

Two months after Evergiste's murder I walked up the path to the entrance of *Les Mille Collines* Hotel in Kigali. We had walked for more than an hour in the flowering gardens of the Hotel. My companion was a high ranking Tutsi official. Without ostentation, he exerted great power. He was said to be the fourth man on the succession list of the Tutsi ruling party.

In a certain way he reminded me of Evergiste. He had the same ability to communicate his innermost feelings to people he barely knew. He had the same eagerness to look into the depths of his torments and to describe what he saw there in unforgettable language.

The Hutu-Tutsi wars never ended. It had expanded into other countries, especially in Burundi and in the Democratic Republic of Congo.

Our conversation was filled at times with long moments of silences, followed by passionate debates. We both knew we were in a labyrinth where truths were elusive, where longings were suppressed, where regrets abounded, where flitting light and darkness appeared and disappeared.

Blaise could be the unifier. He could be the one who would make the deep-rooted hatred between Hutu and Tutsi go away once for all.

He knew I was thinking about what he could do. He shook his head and said: "For a long time after I came back from America, I had a dream, the dream of breaking the vicious circle of killing and revenge. Now I have just enough courage to build a prosperous Rwanda. I am spending all my time to promote industrial progress and agricultural development."

He looked up in the sky and said: "I know though that we breathe in hatred, we move in the miasma of bloodshed. We have repeatedly called for national solidarity. *Their* leaders have also called for unity. We even have a government of national union. But really? We are not going to forget mutual genocides in the foreseeable future."

Before he left, he said: "There will be tens, hundreds, thousands of Evergiste. There must be many, many heroes Hutu and Tutsi, who, like your friend Evergiste, accept to be sacrificed, immolated, if hatred is to be erased from this land."

I held his hand. I felt like I was holding Evergiste's hand again. For a moment, behind Blaise's dark-rimmed eyeglasses, his light skin, his flat stomach and emaciated face, I saw the bulky shape, the large eyes and the rough and dark skin of my friend, my guide and my teacher, Evergiste.

Let's Go to Where the Desert Stops

To Austin, Texas

Let's go to where the desert stops,
Where limestone's white under moonlight
And live oak leaves shine jade-green bright
Over dark twisted trunks where the cliff drops.
Here between emerald lakes
The wanderer lies on the grass under starry sky.
Here the embalmed air shakes
Magnolia trees, while millions of bats swirl by.
Here in springtime we sit among thousands of bluebonnets
And Indian paintbrushes and yellow sweet clovers
While cardinals whistle all around us
And purple martins dive acrobatically
with their wings tucked.
This land is where my heart will be
Its red canyons dotted with large bonsai trees
Its crystal falls, its sienna walls, and its mysteries
Have enchanted thousands, who like me,
Find in it the essence of beauty,
And the wealth and weight of history.

A Self-Defense Militia Volunteer and the Orders from On-High

These events marking the beginning of 1946 are seen through the eyes of one of my cousins in the Hue City self-defense militia. After the Japanese surrendered to the Allies, the French men, women and children who had been in detention since March 9, 1945 were released. The Chinese who came to disarm the Japanese sold some of the guns and rifles they got from the Japanese to the French. In the meantime, with the complicity of the British in the South and the Chinese in the North, the French started their reconquest of Vietnam.

Around three hundred French men battled thousands of Vietnamese regular troops and self-defense militia in Hue. They held on to a few strongholds on Right Bank of the Perfume River, sometimes referred to as the European town, while praying hard for the rescue columns to reach them in time. That series of fighting lasting around two months were later called The First Battle for Hue.

Cousin Minh was a volunteer. He did not need the authorities to conscript him. Actually there was no conscription, and apparently there were no authorities. But the battle of Hue had started and many Vietnamese would have to volunteer, to fight and die, because "we" wanted the French strongholds in Hue to be eliminated before "their" reinforcement troops reached the City.

Minh was a perfect volunteer. His parents, especially his mother hated him. For unfathomable reasons, they treated

133

him like he was a household servant and a hired hand responsible for all the heavy tasks in the family vegetable garden.

Minh didn't mind. He liked to be alone in the garden. Sometimes he stopped working to listen to birdsongs, even though he would receive a beating if his mother caught him "idling".

He risked a beating when he sat in the shade and told us old stories. He seemed to have read all the Chinese historical romances and Chinese *wuxia* novels, and remember every little detail in them.

We could read those books ourselves. But it was far more pleasurable to listen to Minh. He had the innate art of making every scene come alive. We worshipped him and later on I realized that the little circle of eager listeners he drew around him was the greatest solace he found in his life at that time.

*

With the revolution things changed. Rejected suitors of pretty girls in our village came back on horseback, with a sword and a pistol in their belts (*True, unlike the Liberation Army elsewhere, officers in Hue rode horses left behind by the Emperor, the Japanese and the Chinese; they were issued long swords left by the Japanese officers*) . They were now the officers of the new Liberation Army. But the pretty girls remained submissive to their parents who rejected any marriage proposal from non-Catholic suitors. Rejected once again, the suitors rode out of the village, swearing they would never look back.

Cousin Minh surprised us one day when after an absence of a few hours he reappeared in Self-Defense Militia uniform and a sword.

His mother looked with disdain at the wooden scabbard that served as the sheath for his ugly-looking sword and said: "Why don't you have a leather scabbard for your sword?"

To that, Cousin Minh nodded and said: "I am not an officer of the regular army. I am merely a squad leader in the Self-Defense Militia."

No matter, now that he has a sword – that he kept by his side even when he was in bed, his mother had to talk to him with some degree of restraint.

But Cousin Minh needed a circle of listeners around him even more than before. We were his solace whenever he came back from the battlefront: In those days, he used to disappear into the twilight and come home early in the morning to sleep. He would wake up in the afternoon, and told us what had happened the night before. Then at sundown he would go and join his unit again for another night of combat.

We loved his combat narratives far more than the Chinese historical romances and wuxia novels earlier. Through his narratives we could, even at that tender age, see how stupidly the war could be conducted and how tens of thousands of lives could be sacrificed for no purpose at all. And we learned something about the horrendous power of faceless people hiding behind what they so conveniently called *Orders from On-High*.

*

Cousin Minh constantly referred to the orders he received as orders from the *higher ranks* (thượng cấp), later

135

called orders from *On-High.* At first, Cousin Minh said *orders from On-High* in the most reverent way. The reverence he showed to that entity kept increasing even after his squad and then his platoon suffered extremely heavy casualties. Meanwhile other squads and platoons of self-defense militia around his suffered even higher casualties for sticking to the *orders from On-High.*

The daily and nightly rituals never changed during the first Battle for Hue.

A little after sundown all the units of self-defense militia would assemble on the Left Bank of the Perfume River and were handled down a series of *orders from On-High.* Then they all would swim across the river and start their attacks on the few strongholds defended by the French.

The French regained possession of all the buildings on the Right Bank soon after dawn. By that time all the units of self-defense militia would have already left the Right Bank and retreated back to the Left Bank by swimming across the river.

The first casualties were among those who could not swim. And there were a great number of self-defense militiamen who were non-swimmers. But nobody dared disobey the *order from On-High.* So a couple of thousands of non-swimmers drowned on the first night.

The regular troops stood on high ground and contemplated with horror the scene of massive drowning. They eventually stepped forward and offered ropes. Good swimmers would swimmer to the other bank of the river with one end of the ropes; the other end was tied to trees on the Left Bank. Non-swimmers avoided drowning by holding on the ropes until they reached the shallow bottom of the river on the other side.

The second wave of massive casualties occurred when the French started pointing bright search lights on the river and spotting the swimmers long before they reach firm land on the Right Bank.

The regular troops suggested that those crossing the river should push large rafts of water hyacinths before them. At first the French did not see anything wrong with water hyacinths crossing the width of the river. But then they realized that floating water hyacinths normally drifted downstream, eastward, down to the sea. So they sprayed bullets on the water hyacinths and the militiamen who pushed them across the river.

Once they reached the Right Bank, the self-defense militia volunteers would run to their targets. The *orders from On-High* specified that they would swarm over large two- or three-floor buildings brandishing their swords and spears and exterminate the French in those buildings. That's when the third massive wave of casualties occurred. The French were armed with light and heavy machine guns. They usually retreated to the second or third floor, and would come down the stairs from time to time and spray bullets at the militia killing a bunch of then, and then retreat to the higher floor and rest.

There was no way for the militia to rush upstairs as the French would concentrate their fire on the stairs and kill enough to block further attempts with the bodies of dead militia.

Night after night the same rituals played out until the people *On-High* decided on a new strategy to exterminate the French. It took a lot of doing but bales of straw were piled up on the ground floor of the attacked buildings. The French not understanding what was afoot stayed put on the higher floor. An *order from On-High* told the militia to throw large bags of chili pepper on top of the bales of straw, then to set fire on the straw.

It was expected that the French upstairs would come down with their hands up after they were suffocated by the smoke and the intense chili fumes.

What happened was that the French on the higher floors simply opened their windows. The heat and smoke and the chili pepper fumes drove the militia out of the ground floor.

*

After the first wave of casualties, new recruits stepped in to refill the ranks in the decimated squads and platoons. After the second wave, Cousin Minh was made platoon leader. He tried to join the units of the regular army that stayed behind and watched the slaughter to the militia volunteers.

Minh wanted to join the regular units, not because he wanted to stay behind and watch the slaughter of his former comrades-in-arms but because the regulars were relatively better armed. At least they had hand grenades, and every five of them got a rifle.

After the chili pepper episode Cousin Minh started snarling whenever his platoon received an *order from On-High.*

Cousin Minh and his platoon were assigned by the people *On-High* to escort the only battery of 75mm cannon they managed to field in first the Battle for Hue. It was manned by two Japanese former non-commissioned officers, who had preferred to join the Liberation Army than to surrender to the Allied Forces. The Japanese adopted Vietnamese names: one was called Hung (The Bear), the other, Ho (The Tiger). Yet, they were amused immensely whenever they were called by their Vietnamese names.

When Cousin Minh joined the battery, it had only a dozen shells left. *Orders from On-High* told the Japanese to do as much damage to the French as possible with the remaining shells, and to destroy the battery after that.

Cousin Minh said he did not know how much damage a dozen shells could cause. He witnessed the destruction of the only cannon that the Liberation Army got for the Battle of Hue.

Soon enough, the French reinforcement columns arrived in Hue. The first Battle for Hue ended. All the units of the Self Defense Militia were ordered to witness the burning of the Imperial Palace in Hue while all the units of the Liberation regular troops fled to the mountains.

Cousin Minh did not have the heart to witness the destruction of the Palace. He ordered members of his platoon to go home.

He went home and buried his sword.

*

The French crossed the Perfume River and encountered no resistance.

Since that time, whenever he heard a stupid suggestion, recommendation, advice or order he would laugh and say: "Here comes an *order from On-High*".

*

Twenty years later, during the Tet Mau Than Offensive (1968), during the Second Battle for Hue, tens of thousands of Hueans were slaughtered by *orders from On-High*.

*

In 1975, barely 29 years after the first Battle for Hue, millions of South Vietnamese were put into prisons and re-education camps on *orders from On-High.*

At the same time, in Cambodia, over two million innocent people were slaughtered by *orders from On-High,* in one of the most horrible genocides in the history of mankind.

The people who killed under the mask of *people On-High* have been unmasked. And the history of Vietnam and Cambodia will soon be rewritten without the fear of those who created the faceless *On-High.*

*

Cousin Minh was back to telling young kids stories of Chinese historical romances and Chinese *wuxia.* Rarely would he talk about his experiences with the self defense militia. When he did, he sounded both funny and ironic. His most acidic comments were always directed against the *orders from On-High.*

His mother no longer harassed him. She remembered the sword buried a few feet from the back wall of her home.

*

In 1978, a few years after the fall of Saigon, Cousin Minh met a wealthy woman who wanted to make him happy. He was married and lived since then with his wealthy wife in a large villa close to the center of Saigon, now renamed Ho Chi Minh City. He preferred to call it *Minh's City.*

He never left Vietnam, never tried to reach America. He and his wife were never bothered by the new regime. His neighbors in *Minh's City* vaguely referred to him as one of the earlier self-defense militia volunteers, one who had fought the bloody first Battle for Hue.

His wife thought that they would be better off with a certificate proclaiming that he was a hero of the Resistance to the French. Paying the going price for such a certificate was not a problem for the wealthy Mrs. Minh.

These days, as soon as a visitor crosses the threshold of his door, he or she would immediately see hanging on the wall his framed Hero Certificate, with all the red seals and gold and red ribbons.

If a visitor looks a little too long at the Certificate, Cousin Minh would say modestly: "Oh, that's nothing! The first Battle for Hue, you know!"

Whenever we, his cousins, come to see him he would smile and say: "I am a hero now; but I don't receive *orders from On-High* any more. "

The Farmer

Along the way Martin kept calling me "stupid".

Driving across South Africa during the month of January was not fun. Far from it! And having Martin on the passenger seat was no fun either. He never wanted to drive, but seemed to know very well how to drive me crazy with his instructions. For this trip, he kept repeating "You can never learn, can you? I have told you a hundred times already that when you drive a car with the steering wheel on your left, and on a road with left side traffic, a conservative driver like you needs to remember just one thing: *Do everything wrong and you will be all right.*"

I did not resent his calling me "stupid", but "conservative"? Where did that come from?

I had known Martin for many years and had been acquainted to many of his personae. Yea, he had been for a few years an officer in the French Foreign Legion. Then he somehow had managed to become a priest of an adventurous Order, the White Fathers, whose missionary work was narrowly focused on Africa. Was his real name Martin Schultz, or was it merely his Foreign Legion name? For a while I had suspected him of not being a priest at all, until the day he was called to Rome to head an office at the Palazzo San Callisto, or perhaps until I saw him arguing strenuously against the Cardinal, head of his dicastery (*ministry or department* outside of the Vatican).

He invited me to his camp in the "jungle", but there was no jungle in that God-forsaken part of the world. A couple of miles down from his camp were lush fields of corn, irrigated fields. But his camp was set up in the dusty half-desert plot of land that he might have gotten from the local chief for a bottle of wine when the latter was half drunk.

At that camp he organized one seminar after another invariably called "New Leadership Training". He wanted to train a generation of community leaders to serve in the post-apartheid South Africa.

So there we were, driving through the brown and red dust bowls and the lush irrigated fields tended by the Boers or Farmers. Only here even at the time we drove across South Africa to Transvaal, a Boer still was the king, and the Black tenant farmers or farmer hands still were his subjects.

*

The closer we came to his camp, the more taciturn Martin became. I summoned up my courage and asked him in the end: "What's wrong with you?"

He shook his head, remained silent for a long while, then finally sighed and let out:" What I do, what we do is too little, too late. The young men we train will not be leaders in their communities. They would be called *moderates,* an extremely dangerous label in revolutionary times. They will be swept away by a tidal wave of racial hatred. No matter what the National Union Government are doing in Pretoria and Johannesburg, no reconciliation between Whites and Blacks would be able to prevent civil strives, and bloodshed, and the revenge of the oppressed."

*

I walked out of my tent every morning weaker and dirtier. Well water was rationed, and every day we were allowed to wash our face and rub our neck with a wet towel. But no water for a shower! Food was mainly mashed potato and corn on the cob. But we could drink as much as we wanted a weird concoction of coca and South African red table wine. The sugar in the coca kept us going and the bad wine washed away pain and frustration.

I longed to be back in Geneva where food was wholesome and where the streets were clean, and the lawns manicured.

It was then that the Boer or Farmer came to the rescue. One afternoon he sent a driver to our camp and invited both Martin and me to come to his *humble* home for dinner. The driver said: "Please be ready by five. I will be back to take you to the Big House. Dinner will be served at seven, but the Farmer invites you to come early and have a shower before the meal."

"Should we take the second invitation, the invitation to take a shower, to be an insult?" Martin shook his head, thanked the driver profusely and turning to me, he said: "Never refuse what is good! A shower is what we need most. You will not survive two weeks without a shower."

In my mind I heard: "Are we cozying up to the enemy?", as the Famer should be a bloodthirsty tyrant, a mean exploiter of the hundreds of farm hands working and living on his land. But I did not say anything.

*

So we were picked up by five and the driver kept talking about the Boer saying that he was one of the best Farmers in Transvaal. Neither Martin nor I ventured to ask questions concerning grumblings against Boers in general, and the Black resentment that seeped even into our seminar.

As we drove through miles of irrigated fields I was reminded of something I had seen in Madras three decades earlier.

One evening I was also driven to the mansion of Governor of Madras. It took us precisely twenty minutes at fairly good speed to cover the distance from the gate to steps at the entrance of the mansion. Meanwhile we went past successive flower gardens, each with its own specific color, yellow, golden, purple, bright red, creamy white then a huge wildlife park where elephants and deer roamed. On that evening I saw with my mind's eyes the true "holes in the wall" where the very poor in Madras lived amidst hundreds of thousands of hungry and screeching black crows.

No, *the Big House* was not *that* big! Strangely enough, the Boer and his wife met us at the steps of the entrance. Pete Brinkerhoff in his regular fit white sport shirt and straight leg twill pants shook hands and insisted that we called him simply Pete; which we did.

Kim, his wife was ravishing in her impeccably tailored seaside chambray shirt and silky faux wrap skirt. Their very young daughters, Mila and Reiko -- maybe eleven and nine -- wore stunning golden Youngland eyelash organza dresses. Once inside, they ran away and came back with two piles of soft and thick towels. Mila said to Martin: "You may need these." Reiko simply thrust the towels into my arm, laughed and ran away again.

Martin was quite at ease with the whole family: He had been saying mass at the family chapel every Sunday (on weekdays he said mass at the camp). He gave socialistic homilies to the whole congregation, the Brinkerhoffs and their tenant farmers, farmhands and their families.

The long shower was energizing, yet I found myself wondering. The perfection of the welcoming, the expected perfect meal did not dispel my vague apprehension of what could happen in the near future to that beautiful family. I tried to chase away my dark thoughts but my mind was a battlefield where my anger over twenty years of apartheid and the colonization days dating back to the 17th century that had been the cause of untold pain to the Blacks and my terror at the thought of the upcoming campaign against the Whites.

It was in a pensive mood that I partook with my hosts a simple but splendid meal rich in rituals, rich in Dutch flavors, from the pickled Holland matjes (young) herrings, to the stamppot of kale, spinach and turnip green mixed with sausage and lardons, the ossenhaas or beef tenderloin, the Edam cheese and the apple rings and almond sticks.

The simplicity and the smooth flowing from one course to another, with the choreography of servants who listened to the conversation at the table and burst out laughing at times without causing our hosts to frown.

That air of camaraderie and even complicity between our hosts and their household staff did not assuage my fear for the future. I was so pensive that at the moment Pete and Kim and their daughters accompanied us to the car Pete said softly to me: "Don't you worry for us, dear friend. We will be all right no matter what happens in the future."

So, Pete had read my thoughts. But was he able to read the writing on the wall? Was he a prophet? Was he endowed with the gift of prophecy? Or was he simply an optimist fool?

Kim said: "See you tomorrow at mass."

*

The next morning we walked to the chapel of the plantation. While Martin went in to get robed, I stood outside and watched the colorful stream of farm hands, their wives and their children going up the hill to mass. I saw the Farmer drove his family to the foot of the hill and stopped there. He walked briskly with his wife, talking and laughing with them while their daughters ran to the children their age among the black families and ran together laughing and screaming excitedly. It was eerie to watch the scene when your mind already saw what would happen a few years away.

Kim and Pete Brinkerhoff stopped and talked with me a couple of minutes then turned around to greet one family after another as they entered the chapel.

At mass, Reiko and Mila, at the right moment, collected the Sunday offerings, handling the baskets-on-a- stick almost professionally—almost, as they sometimes giggled after bowing their heads to thank those who dropped some money into the baskets.

After mass, Reiko and Mila ran again with girls their age, laughing, screaming and giggling happily while Pete and Kim talked with farmhands seriously about weather and the lack of rain.

Martin was so perceptive that he stopped me on our walk back to the camp. He asked: "What's wrong?"

I did not answer; and he nodded: "Is this too idyllic? Are you afraid that this would not last? *Carpe diem,* seize the day! So said Horace! Enjoy the moment. The rest is in God's hand."

I knew that he like me had seen whole worlds disappear in front of our eyes. I said:" I don't need a sermon. What I need is a full glass of your awful concoction (Red South African

147

table wine on Coca-Cola). Martin laughed: "Nope. Today we will enjoy good beer from Holland. Last night Pete loaded a whole case of Heineken onto the jeep. Enjoy what is good, my friend"

*

It was a rainy day in Geneva. My staff was all gone. I sat in my large and lonely office. I did not want to go home. It was five years after that night at the Brinkerhoffs.

What I had seen with my mind's eyes had become reality. Nightmarish fires started by arsonists, broken down doors, smashed in windows, blood stains on the floors and on the walls, bloated bodies of violated and slaughtered women, bodies of men covered with hundreds of stab wounds.

I closed my mind against the tragedy unfolding. Yet I knew what happened to isolated Farmers had happened to tens of thousands black men and women during 20 years of apartheid and decades of colonization before that.

I couldn't pick up Boer magazines that kept coming in from South Africa every Thursday. But that day, I caught the names Brinkerhoffs on the cover of the magazine. I went numb. It took me several hours before I could summon all my courage to read the story.

No, I wanted to see Kim and Pete talk excitedly about weather with their black farm hands. I wanted to see Reiko and Mila run with black girls their age, laughing, screaming and giggling happily... That was the real world. The horror world that came to replace it was as unreal as my nightmares.

I sat in my large and lonely office and said to God:" Tell me that this is not true!"

148

I knew that Martin still was in his small office at Palazzo San Callisto, he would be there every day until the maintenance crew came and literally kicked him out of there. I had to call him even though that was the last thing I wanted to do. I did not want a confirmation of what I had read.

Martin hated to pick up the phone when he worked after hours. He had told me that if he stayed far into the evening, it was because he needed to work without being disturbed.

So the phone kept ringing for a long while before I heard the click and he said angrily: *"Pronto"*

He recognized my voice after a few words and said: "So, you have read the article?" We did not need to say whom we were talking about.

I asked: "Yes. Is it true that they are all dead?"

He was silent for a while then said:" The farm was ravaged. Their mansion was burned down. But did they die? We don't know."

I screamed at him: "Don't give me false hopes!"

He was silent again. Then he said: "Reasonably speaking, they must be dead, all of them. But as you know, Boer magazines are exaggerating sometimes. We have our sources of course, but what we have gotten are contradictory stories."

He said *"we"* like he was part now of the grand network of the Holy See, an incomparable network that gathers information from the grassroots, to the diocesan, the national, regional and international levels. I hated him for it, and on that day I hated him more than others, because he had broken ranks with us, the field operators, and become part of a bureaucracy, even a bureaucracy that could provide me the needed information.

I sighed: "Give me the truth. I can take it."

He became apologetic: "I must not give you false hopes, of course. I will say a mass for the rest of their souls after tomorrow. Will you come?"

It would be a short flight from Geneva to Rome. I used to go to Rome for less important events. But, this time, I decided not to go.

*

It was a day in April. I was in the middle of the splendor of Keukenhof during the season of tulip blooming. Watching the crowd of tourists around me, I wondered how many of them only came for the tulips, how many came to see the people who generation after generation worked to reclaim land from the sea.

I remembered Pete de Haas who was my best man at our wedding in Paris thirty years earlier. Pete must be living in Enschede now. Somehow my wife and I had lost track of him since his return to Holland, though we still kept religiously as memento a Delf blue porcelain plate, his wedding gift. At the Sorbonne where we were studying, Pete was talking non-stop about the resilience and determination of the Dutch, and how they conquered the sea. I tried to focus on Peter de Haas so that my mind would not be led to the face of another Pete.

I was standing in Keukenhof with the tulips blooming around me wondering when exactly the sea was finally drained out of the land I stood on. "Dutch conquered not only the sea and the swamps, Peter de Hass said, they also conquered the desert in South Africa. Irrigation and determination had created hundreds of plantations in Zimbabwe and in South Africa".

For a few second the splendor of Keukenhof disappeared. Images of the attacks on Dutch farms surged in my mind and left me stranded in devastated fields and mansions. My eyes blurred.

Then they were no longer blurred. Even from behind I could recognize that head, that neck, those shoulders. I shouted "Pete". It was Pete Brinkerhoff.

"No, this is impossible. He died last year in Transvaal." I said to myself.

Pete turned around, froze, and then ran toward me.

We hugged until our hugging seemed to disturb the crowd. Pete said:" Let's go to my home. Kim, Reiko and Mila will be thrilled to see you."

*

It was not as spacious as their *Big House* in South Africa, but the home Pete and Kim had bought in Keukenhof was more than adequate for a family of four. The guest rooms were not stylish but well furnished and decorated.

Kim decreed: "You will stay with us a couple of day, won't you?"

I nodded. I still was in a daze. Here Mila came with a thick pile of towels, thrust them at me and said: "You may need these for your shower". She burst laughing and ran away.

Pete said: "Forgive her. She hasn't forgotten a single detail about your visit in Transvaal".

I said: "Maybe before I take a shower we should call Martin and let him know that I have found you here safe and sound. Please make the call. Here is his number in Rome."

The telephone call was a success. At first Martin was too stunned to talk. But soon enough he was dancing around in his small office at the Palazzo San Callisto. When Pete put us all on the speakerphone Reiko and Mila started an improvised hip hop and answered Martin question in short and rhymed sentences.

After the phone call we looked at one another. The shower could wait.

With Kim smiling and the girls giggling, and Pete talking like he was never going to stop, I was rarely so happy in my life.

*

It did not take Kim and the girls too much time to whip up a royal dinner. Pete took me to the backyard. Sitting comfortably in large wicker armchairs we talked and talked over a couple of bottles of Heineken.

Pete said: "We were, Kim and I, were guilty of imprudence. We should have gotten out much earlier. Our escape was quite a miracle. Concretely, we were saved by the farm hands. They warned us a couple of days before the attack on our plantation. They put us on a van and said: "Get out of here."

With his head hung low he added: "So far they are doing quite well even after the plantation was partly destroyed. They keep me informed about the situation over there. I have been able to send them medicine, seeds and money to help the most distressed among them. But that does not stop the sense of guilt in me. I will carry with me for long years the guilt for abandoning ship!"

I told him: "If you had stayed on what good could come out of that? Your farm hands would be forced to betray you or to share your ordeal".

He smiled and said: "You are right."

I asked: "Was it difficult for you to restart your life here?"

He shook his head, but did not say anything for a while. Finally he said: "My father was born in South Africa, I was born in Africa. Kim was born here in The Netherlands. I met her over there when she came to Dunbar to see her uncle. And we got married in a hurry. So South Africa is my native land...But then, Holland is Kim's native land. No, we did not find it difficult to restart our life here. We bought at a land here for half the going price from Kim's father. And we started cultivating bulbs.

*

The meal was elaborately Dutch. We drank *juniper* with lager beer as chaser. The glasses of juniper (Dutch gin) were fresh out of the freezers, and we couldn't hold them in our hand at first. We had to drink the first sip of the icy liquid by bending our back and applying our mouth to the glasses. The girls looked on with amusement and stayed with their glasses of water.

Inevitably raw herring and *rookworst* or smoked sausages were on the menu. Braised beef and mashed potato followed. Lemon cakes concluded the meal.

During the meal I couldn't help but notice that South Africa had put dark circles around Pete's and Kim's eyes and that even the girls had aged and had turned into introspective young ladies, fully aware of their new environment and of the precariousness of their past life.

*

We went to the living room after dinner for more chatting. A short moment later the telephone rang. It was Johannes Van Leibbrandt and two other former Farmers who wanted to come and have a drink with the Brinkerhoffs.

Sensing tension I wanted to excuse myself. But both Kim and Pete told me I should meet their unexpected visitors.

Soon enough we heard a jeep stop right at the front door. The front door was promptly opened by a maid, and three tall men wearing heavy boots strode in.

Pete stood up to shake hand, with some hesitation. He turned to me and introduced the new arrival:" This is Johannes Van Leibbrandt, this is Liam Dekker and this is Lars Jaager". Kim seemed to be slightly distressed and the girls were icily polite. Kim asked the girls to say goodnight and go up to their rooms. The girls complied gratefully.

Johannes apologized for dropping by unexpectedly but said he had received more news from Transvaal. His "news" was no news as he simply repeated what the most aberrant Boer magazines had reported for weeks about the vandalism and inhuman cruelty of Black gangs.

Pete turned to me: "Johannes was in a sense our neighbor. His plantation was fifteen miles south of our home." I nodded: "Yes, I did hear about Mr. Van Leibbrandt when I was in Transvaal."

Johannes glanced at me a second then returned his gaze on Kim.

Pete said: "Johannes may tell you how he escaped from there."

Johannes said proudly: "I fought my way out. My wife, our son and me, we shot down ten or maybe twenty of *them* before we jumped into a jeep and sped out of there."

The three visitors laughed boisterously. Pete, Kim and I couldn't see anything funny in that, so we just looked at them uncertainly.

Liam Dekker said: "We were here on vacation when they attacked our plantation. So we couldn't save anything at all. Our butler and our foreman were killed by those rabid dogs."

Lars Jaager added: "They never attacked our place. We will wait a little then when the situation looks better we will go back."

Both Johannes and Liam said in unison: "The situation will never improve for White Farmers!"

Neither the Brinkerhoffs nor I tried to keep the conversation going after that. And after a while Johannes, Liam and Lars understood they were not welcome to stay. Their exit was as noisy as his arrival.

Pete said after the jeep was gone: "Maybe we should not open the door to them anymore." Kim sighed: "You are right. Johannes always gives me the creeps."

"Apparently life is precarious wherever we live", I thought. "Everywhere the threat on our tranquility is real."

*

Two wonderful days later, as I was leaving, I asked Pete: "Have you ever thought of going back over there?

Pete laughed but he looked somewhat melancholy when he said: "No. I am an optimistic fool but I know when a world ends and another begins".

The Crescent Moon there in the Sky

To Sagrario

The crescent moon there in the sky,

Dark clouds that sail over the slumbering hills,

Oh let me say before I die

How much there is in a short life.

Let me close my eyes and tell you what this single night

Has brought in to my soul and my mind.

Surrounded by wet and familiar fragrance

Of night-scented flowers I sit

In your secret garden where dimly lit

Limestone glimmers in the starlight.

My cup has been full to the brim, always been,

My joy has overwhelmed sweat and toil and fear.

Even now when the twilight has gone, my dear

We breathe the same air in this secret garden

Crafted by years of wordless communication

And that's enough. Or is it?

I know there are countries our eyes haven't seen.

I know there are mountain streams we haven't crossed.

A few books we haven't read and commented upon

A few strands of thought we somehow have lost,

Interrupted by a greeting or a smile.

I believe that a child still is hungry somewhere

I believe we still ought to be there.

But life is wonderful in that

The child will be fed by others

Or maybe she dies and suffers no more.

My eyes are heavy with sleep;

Yet my mind hasn't stopped wandering

And meandering.

Until we find a few answers to our quest

And a place where we really want to rest.

Then I will look at you, inhaling deeply the fragrance

And the mellowness of *that* scented garden

I will hold your hand with deep reverence

And say: "what a life

I've had, with you by my side!"

About ANDRÉ NGUYỄN VĂN CHÂU

Andre Nguyen Van Chau was born in the Citadel of Hue, the old capital of Imperial Vietnam. He grew up with classmates who have become known writers, poets, composers and painters.

After obtaining a doctorate degree in the humanities at the Sorbonne, Paris, he taught English and creative writing at various universities in Viet Nam for twelve years.

In 1975 he began twenty-five years of work for migrants and refugees around the world, ten of which were spent at the head of the International Catholic Migrations Commissions with 84 national affiliates and with headquarters in Geneva, Switzerland.

He has traveled and worked in over 90 countries.

Back to the United States after Geneva he was for ten years the Director, Language and Accent Training at ACS, then Xerox before retiring in Austin, Texas and beginning a new career as a full-time writer.

One of his published works, *The Miracle of Hope,* has been translated into nine different languages.

The New Vietnamese-English Dictionary, on which he spent an inordinate number of hours in the last twenty years, was finally published in 2014.

He and his wife, Sagrario, have four children: Andrew, married to Jodie Scales, Boi-Lan, married to Rodolphe Lemoine, Michael, married to Rachel La Fleur and Xavier. They have seven grand-children: Katleyn, Géraldine, Alix, Drew, Noah, Isabelle and Luke.

Other Books By This Author

A Lifetime in the Eye of the Storm

History is colored by the nation that is recording it. In America, the Vietnam War was chronicled in the newspapers and on television. The heart breaking stories we heard were always about the war from the American viewpoint. When we are able to view historical events from perspectives other than our own, we begin to understand that the important thing isn't winning or losing, but learning and understanding.

Hiep lived her life, from earliest childhood, at the center of the war. This is her story of love and loss, triumph and tragedy. It is the story of all women who have lived through a war, with only their steadfast love, hope and faith in God to give them the strength to go on living.

"A moving account of the Ngo Dinh family's determination to live and work for the freedom of their beloved country."

The Miracle of Hope

Known to many Catholics through his writings (Testimony of Hope; The Road of Hope), Vietnam's late Cardinal Francis Xavier Nguyen Van Thuan's amazing story is told by a former fellow seminarian who knew him from the time the cardinal was 18. Chau initially declined the cardinal's request to write about his life, but in 1999, reluctantly agreed, finishing the book just a few months before the cardinal died in 2002. Chau has meticulously chronicled Cardinal Thuan's life and that of his prominent family, which paid dearly for its involvement in the quest for Vietnam's independence. To help the reader navigate through a complex cast of characters, Chau has included a glossary and an explanation of Vietnamese personal names. He portrays Cardinal Thuan as a humble man who gladly would have served as a rural pastor, but was marked for leadership in the church early on. Even as he prepared for this role studying in Europe, Cardinal Thuan had a premonition that he would suffer martyrdom, and indeed, after being named coadjutor archbishop of Saigon in 1975, he was arrested by Communist authorities. Thuan subsequently spent 13 years in prison, which shaped his spirituality and leadership. ~ *Publishers Weekly*

The New Vietnamese - English Dictionary

This is an advanced Vietnamese dictionary with English definitions, compiled with the enrichment of the Vietnamese language in mind.

This dictionary lists words and expressions used by Vietnamese throughout the ages. It shows local and ethnic dialectal words and phrases and promotes the understanding of the Vietnamese culture past and present.

Over 1170 pages – the most comprehensive collection to date.